Tanner picked up the handcuff and slapped it around Maddie's wrist

"Gotcha," he said with a satisfied, sexy grin.

"This is silly," Maddie protested weakly as the heat in Tanner's gaze uncoiled something deep inside her. Flustered, she turned and picked up the key from the nightstand. "All I have to do is unlock it...." Her voice trailed off when she realized the key wouldn't turn.

"You look so sexy in red," Tanner teased, running his finger along her arm.

Goose bumps broke out along her skin and Maddie sucked in a deep breath, trying in vain to gather her scattered wits. She licked her lips. "Don't do this to me, Tanner."

Tanner brushed a tendril of hair off her cheek. "You're under the mistaken impression that I'm some kind of Casanova. I'm not. But ever since we met, there's been something between us...."

"Tanner, we can't..." She moaned as he shifted his weight on the bed, bringing him closer—intimately closer. "No matter how much I'd like to," she gasped.

"Maddie," he said, dropping a soft kiss on her lips, "I don't think you're in a position to argue...."

Dear Reader,

I had so much fun with my first Temptation novel—
writing about a strapping, sexy hero and the strong,
sassy woman who catches him. And in my book, that's
exactly what my heroine, Maddie Griffin, does. You
see, Maddie is an aspiring bounty hunter and she takes
her job very seriously. So when Tanner Blackburn
proves to be too dangerously irresistible for the women
of the world, Maddie is determined to keep the female
population safe. One way or another...

I'd love to hear what you think of Maddie and Tanner's
amorous escapades. You can reach me online at
www.KristinGabriel.com or write to me at P.O. Box
5162, Grand Island, NE 68801-5162.

Enjoy,

Kristin Gabriel

Books by Kristin Gabriel

HARLEQUIN LOVE & LAUGHTER
40—BULLETS OVER BOISE
56—MONDAY MAN
62—SEND ME NO FLOWERS

HARLEQUIN DUETS
 7—ANNIE, GET YOUR GROOM
25—THE BACHELOR TRAP
27—BACHELOR BY DESIGN
29—BEAUTY AND THE BACHELOR

DANGEROUSLY IRRESISTIBLE
Kristin Gabriel

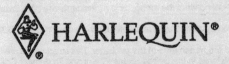

HARLEQUIN®

TORONTO • NEW YORK • LONDON
AMSTERDAM • PARIS • SYDNEY • HAMBURG
STOCKHOLM • ATHENS • TOKYO • MILAN • MADRID
PRAGUE • WARSAW • BUDAPEST • AUCKLAND

For you, Kent.

ISBN 0-373-25934-4

DANGEROUSLY IRRESISTIBLE

Copyright © 2001 by Kristin Eckhardt.

Visit us at www.eHarlequin.com

Printed in U.S.A.

____Prologue____

MADDIE GRIFFIN STOOD on her tiptoes to peek through the grimy window of the double-wide trailer. She saw green shag carpet on the living room floor, a centerfold hanging on the wall, and a shotgun propped in the corner—right next to the young man sprawled in a recliner with a can of beer in his hand.

He was tall and wiry, with fuzz on his chin that barely passed for a goatee. Not more than eighteen, he wore ragged denim cutoffs and a sweat-stained gray T-shirt with a gaping hole under one arm.

Maddie moved away from the window, her heart racing in her chest as she prepared to put her plan into action.

Retrieving a smoke bomb from her bag, she lit it, then rolled it underneath the souped-up green Chevy Nova sedan parked in the gravel driveway. Plumes of thick grayish-white smoke soon swirled up through the grill and around the front tires of the vehicle.

Crouching behind a dented aluminum trash can,

Maddie pulled out her cell phone and dialed up the occupant of the trailer.

After three rings, a sluggish voice came over the line. "Yeah?"

"Hi, this is Tina, your next-door neighbor." Maddie held her breath, hoping she sounded like the blond bombshell who lived in a nearby trailer. She'd never actually met the woman, though she had nosed through her mailbox to discover her name.

"Hey, Tina," he said, sounding surprised. "What's up?"

"Well, I just looked out my window...and I think your car is on fire."

A moment later, Maddie saw a shadow at his trailer window, then heard a crude oath explode over the line. The telltale squeak of the trailer's front door told her he'd taken the bait.

Obviously, he fit the young and stupid category, as did most of the bail jumpers who kept the Griffin Bail Enforcement Agency so busy.

She stood up and pulled a canister of pepper spray out of her pocket. Her prey raced down the concrete steps toward the car, completely unaware that his freedom was just about to come to an end.

Suddenly, someone tackled Maddie from behind, knocking her into the dirt. The pepper spray went flying as she gasped to regain her breath. She lay flat on her stomach, the crushing weight of the body still on top of her. Before she could scream, a beefy hand clamped over her mouth.

"Shut up or you'll ruin everything, you nitwit!"

Tate. Her big brother had lousy timing. White-hot fury rolled through her as she lifted her head just far enough to see her other brother Ben apprehend the fugitive. *Her* fugitive. The takedown was quick and easy, just as she'd known it would be.

By the time the kid was in handcuffs, Tate had hauled her to her feet and was brushing leaves and grass out of her hair.

Ben strolled up to them, the fugitive in tow. "Damn it, Tate, why did you knock her down like that? You know Dad will chew both our butts if Maddie has even so much as a scratch on her."

"She was holding pepper spray. If you think I'm taking a chance on her spraying me again, you're nuts. Besides, you got the easy part. She bit me!" He held up his palm to show his brother the damage. Then he scowled at Maddie. "I thought you were against violence."

"That's what you get for sneaking up on me! Which, for your information, is the reason I accidentally sprayed you the last time." She wrenched her arm out of her brother's grasp, furious with them both for botching her takedown. Again. "When are you two going to quit following me around?"

"Hey, we're just following Dad's orders." Ben

shook his head. "And you're in trouble this time, sis. Big trouble."

An hour later, Maddie knew her brother hadn't been exaggerating. She stood in her father's office, her ears ringing from the decibel level of his voice. He'd been shouting at her for the past fifteen minutes. Surely he couldn't hold out much longer.

"This is it!" Gus Griffin banged his fist on the desk. "This is the last straw. If I can't trust you to stay in the office, then you're fired. I'll find another secretary."

"Good," she retorted, when he finally paused for breath. "I never wanted to be your secretary. I want to be a bounty hunter, just like you and Ben and Tate. I may not have your brawn, but I've got more than enough brains to do the job, plus a degree in criminal justice from Northwestern. I'm ready."

He narrowed his eyes. "And I'm ready to lock you up until you come to your senses. A lady doesn't belong in this business. And I'm not letting any daughter of mine out on the streets to confront dangerous felons."

She leaned forward, planting both palms on his desk. "Then I'll go work for someone else. Or start my own agency. I'm twenty-five years old, Dad. You can't tell me what to do anymore."

A muscle twitched in his grizzled jaw and Maddie knew that her father was still frustrated that he couldn't control her. That was one of the reasons he'd sent her off to boarding school shortly after her mother's death when she was twelve. He could handle the rough and tumble world of boys, but the thought of dealing with a little girl clearly hadn't appealed to him. So he'd shut her out of the family.

Just like he was doing now.

"You're not working for anyone else," Gus said. "You're going back to school and learn how to be a teacher, or even better, a nurse. Then maybe you'll learn how dangerous it is to bite your brother."

She refused to feel guilty since she hadn't even broken the skin. "This is the third time Ben and Tate have interfered with one of my cases."

His nostrils flared. "You don't have cases! You're a secretary. You're supposed to be filing and making coffee, not shopping for a stun gun."

A blush crept up her cheeks. "You know about that?"

"Yes." He reached into a desk drawer and pulled out a magazine, tossing it on top of the desk. "I also know about this."

The flush deepened as she stared at the title. *Texas Mail-Order Men.* Her friend Shayna Walters had given her a subscription to the magazine as a joke after Maddie had complained that her brothers always scared away any potential suitors. She'd spent more than one lonely Saturday night leafing through the magazine and marking the pages with the best-looking men. She hadn't intended to actually follow through and send for one—no matter how titillating the prospect of pairing up with a perfect stranger might be.

From the expression on her father's face, she wisely kept that opinion to herself. Squaring her shoulders, she decided the best defense was a good offense. "Ben and Tate broke into my apartment again, didn't they? That's an invasion of privacy. They had no right...."

"They had every right," Gus interjected, his thick, gray brows crashing together, "especially when I discovered that you were out pursuing another felon. They were looking for some clue to see where you'd gone—only they found this instead."

Gus opened the magazine to the first dog-eared page and read the caption below the photograph of a half-naked bull rider. *"Eight seconds is all you'll need to know this cowboy is the stud for you."*

He turned to the next dog-eared page. A grinning, naked cowboy held a saddle on his lap, strategically concealing a certain portion of his anatomy. *"Let this cowboy take you for the ride of your life."*

"I can explain," she began, her cheeks hot.

He folded his arms across his burly chest. "I'm waiting."

"I never had any intention of contacting those men."

"So why did you mark the pages?"

She couldn't believe they were sitting here discussing this stupid magazine instead of her career. "It's not like I'd planned to track them down. Although I could," she added, tipping up her chin, "if I wanted to. I'm a damn good tracker, Dad. If you'd just give me a chance...."

"Forget it. No daughter of mine is going to associate with the kind of low-life riffraff who jump bail, especially when you refuse to even carry a gun."

"I carry pepper spray in case I have any problems. And I'm willing to use a stun gun in an emergency." She stood up. "Just because I don't break down doors and wrestle felons to the ground doesn't mean I can't do the job."

He shook his head. "Women don't belong in this business. Look what happened to Lynette."

She rolled her eyes. Lynette had once worked as a secretary at the Griffin Bail Enforcement Agency. She'd also broken Gus Griffin's heart. "Your fiancée ran off with a con artist, Dad, she didn't die in the line of duty."

His gaze flicked to the bulletin board on the wall. Straight to the wanted poster of the man who, one year ago, had stolen the woman he'd loved. The only woman he'd ever considered marrying after her mother's death. But Lynette had dumped him for a man ten years her junior. A man they now knew as the Kissing Bandit. Guilty of fraud and bigamy in three states, the Kissing Bandit had romanced Lynette out of every penny in her savings account, then left her high and dry. He'd been arrested soon after, then jumped bail and disappeared.

Gus Griffin had never forgiven Lynette for jilting him. He'd also vowed to bring the notorious Kissing Bandit to justice. But despite his diligence, the Bandit was still on the loose. And Maddie was still paying the price for Lynette's weakness.

"Maddie, I'm sorry to say that this magazine is proof that you're not ready to hire on as a bounty hunter. It shows poor judgment. You're obviously more interested in romance than recovering fugitives."

"That's not fair! Ben and Tate spend every weekend with a different woman, and you never say a word."

"That's because Ben and Tate have already proven themselves in the field. They're not going to let a pretty face distract them at a crucial moment."

"So give me a chance to prove myself, too. That's all I ask, Dad. One chance."

He hesitated, and for one brief moment she let herself hope.

"Madeline..." he began.

She closed her eyes, knowing the answer even before he said it. Her father never used her full name unless he was about to deliver bad news. He'd called her Madeline when he'd told her about her mother's death in a traffic accident all those years ago. And then again a few months later, when he'd announced that she'd be attending a boarding school in Boston, instead of staying with the family in Chicago.

Madeline had never boded well.

"It's time to put this silly idea out of your head," Gus said gruffly. "You're not going to work for me as a bounty hunter, and you're not going to work for the competition, either. Everybody in this city knows better than to cross Gus Griffin."

"Then I'll open my own business," she said, mortified to feel her lower lip quiver.

"Nobody in their right mind would ever hire a woman to bring in a fugitive, especially a woman who refuses to carry a gun." He stood up and awkwardly thrust a tissue in her direction. Gus Griffin could face an armed felon without blinking an eye, but a woman in tears terrified him.

She grabbed the tissue and wiped her nose, aware of the office door closing behind her. She was alone. Again. Despite the tightness in her throat, her eyes were dry and hot. He wouldn't even give her chance. After all these years, he still wouldn't let her be part of the family.

She'd grown up trying to knock down the emotional wall that kept her separated from her father and brothers. They loved her and tried to protect her, but they didn't understand her. And they didn't want to let her into their world.

She reached across the desk for another tissue, her elbow bumping the magazine onto the floor. With an irritated sigh, she picked it up and scowled at the sexy cowboy who grinned up at her.

"It's all your fault," she muttered, though she knew her father would have used any excuse to keep her safely behind a desk instead of out in the field.

She flipped through the magazine, half tempted to place an order just to irritate her father. She knew it was immature and irrational, but so far acting mature and rational hadn't gotten her very far.

She dropped the magazine into her lap, the pages falling open to the special insert called *Grooms-to-Go*. She'd never looked at this section before, having no interest in a man desperate enough to advertise himself for marriage. Then she blinked at the picture in front of her. And for one brief, terrifying moment her heart fluttered in her chest.

She held her breath as she looked up at the wanted poster in the center of the bulletin board. The one that had been there for so many months. The one with the picture of the Kissing Bandit. Then she looked back at the magazine.

It was him.

Maddie gulped, trying to breathe normally again. She'd found him. The man her father and brothers had been fruitlessly searching for was right here in black and white. His hair was a little shorter, and dark instead of blond, and he'd shaved off his mustache. But he still had the same square jaw, the same sexy dimple in his chin. She quickly scanned the brief description. *Height: Six feet two inches. Hair: Brown. Eyes: Blue. Name: Tanner Blackburn.*

Maddie stood up, too excited to remain still. Tanner Blackburn was one of the aliases of the Kissing Bandit. His name and hair color might change, but his m.o. was always the same. He'd dupe lonely women into falling in love with him, then he'd bleed them dry.

Now the Kissing Bandit was here, right in front of her. Or rather, in Texas. And obviously up to his old tricks. If she could bring him in....

If? *When* she brought him in. Then she'd finally have everything she'd always wanted. The love and respect of her father. The approval of her brothers. The satisfaction of finally proving herself as a full-fledged member of the Griffin family.

She smiled at the photo of the handsome man in the magazine. He'd soon learn that a Griffin always gets her man.

"BREATHE," TANNER BLACKBURN ordered the man standing next to him. "It's just the wedding rehearsal. You don't need to start panicking until tomorrow."

"I'm not panicking," Cabe White said, his voice husky with emotion. "I just can't get over how damn beautiful she is."

They stood in the center of an old barn located on the outskirts of Abilene, Texas. The open doors did little to assuage the oppressive June heat. Flies buzzed around them and the air was ripe with the odors of hay and manure.

Tanner watched as the bride-to-be stood in the doorway. She wore a long pink denim skirt and a pale pink western blouse with pearl buttons. Her fine, silky blond hair was tucked beneath a straw cowboy hat adorned with a pink satin band.

Despite the heat and the flies and the way his new cowboy boots were pinching his toes, Tanner felt a twinge of envy deep inside of him. Cabe and Hannah were meant for each other, even though he'd seen her first. Hell, he'd dated her first. After reluctantly allowing his kid sister to place his picture in the *Texas Mail-Order Men* magazine, he'd finally met a woman who had stirred his interest. He'd thought it was fate.

Until she'd fallen in love with his cousin.

Tanner hadn't even seen Cabe for almost five years. As teenagers, Cabe, Tanner and Tanner's twin brother, Ronnie, had all been hell-raisers together, breaking curfew and female hearts on a regular basis. They'd all had the same dark hair, deep blue eyes, and square Blackburn jaw that the ladies seemed to love. And they had all loved the ladies.

But Tanner had given up his playboy ways after his parents divorced when he was twenty-four years old. He'd even agreed to take custody of his kid sister, Lauren, who at fourteen, had been well on her way to becoming the most notorious hell-raiser of all.

Cabe and Ronnie hadn't grown up as much as drifted away. Except for a card at Christmas, they rarely kept in touch. They hadn't even attended their maternal grandmother's funeral. Tanner had been named executor of the estate and contacted each of them about their inheritance. He, Ronnie and Lauren had been given eighty acres of Iowa farmland that had been in the family for three generations. Their cousin Cabe had inherited their grandmother's house in Hominy, Iowa. A month ago, Cabe had come to Dallas to collect the deed.

That's when he'd met Hannah.

And that's when fate had decided to play a trick on Tanner. Hannah had taken one look at Cabe and fallen hard and fast. It had been love at first sight for both of them. Hell, even Tanner had seen that. They'd both politely waited to act on their affection until Tanner had offered to step aside.

What else could he do? Hannah wanted someone who could sweep her off her feet. A man who would think it was romantic to marry western-style in an old dilapidated barn.

A man the exact opposite of Tanner Blackburn.

He'd realized that he'd almost made a big mistake. Hannah was a nice woman, but she wasn't the right woman. Not for him. He wasn't even sure such a woman existed, but he intended to keep looking. Instead of heading home for Dallas, he'd bought an airplane ticket to Jamaica. With over ten weeks in vacation time built up, Tanner thought it was time for a little rest and relaxation. And, if he was lucky, a little romance.

It had taken some juggling to arrange a week off from his job at the law firm of Collins and Cooksey, but he'd refused to put it off. This was the first vacation he'd had since... Well, he couldn't remember when. Vacations were a luxury his parents hadn't been able to afford, especially after their divorce.

By the time Tanner had worked his way through college and law school, he'd been too busy paying off his school loans to take any time off. Plus, he'd wanted to keep an eye on his sister.

All of which hadn't left him much time for a love life.

But his little sister had graduated from high school this year and was leaving for college in the fall, which meant he'd be on his own. That was one of the reasons he'd agreed to let Lauren place his picture in the *Texas Mail-Order Men* magazine. It was just a lark, though he'd felt duty bound to go out on a date with every woman who contacted him.

All thirty-four of them.

The problem was, most of them weren't looking for love. Not really. They wanted a knight in shining armor. Someone to rescue them from the jerks in their lives—men who preyed on a woman's vulnerabilities.

Men like his brother, Ronnie—although Ronnie had recently turned over a new leaf. He was now a missionary in Guam, of all places. The former bronc rider, once coined the Romeo of the rodeo, now kept himself busy doing good deeds. Tanner wasn't totally convinced by his brother's abrupt metamorphosis from playboy to preacher. Still, he'd been gone for the past few months and showed no sign of returning.

Now Tanner was ready for a change, too. He'd had enough of bachelor life and was ready to settle down. The hard part seemed to be finding the right woman. After his recent experiences on the dating scene, he longed for a woman who desired him. Just him. Not his bank account. Or his handyman abilities. Or his new Chevy Tahoe SUV.

He had high hopes of finding his fantasy woman in Jamaica. Strolling along a white sand beach in a string bikini. A woman with a thirst for banana daiquiris and making love in the moonlight. A woman who liked the thrill of the chase and could give him something that had been missing in his life for far too long—a challenge.

A horse whinnied in the stall behind him, reminding Tanner to pay attention to the wedding rehearsal. The minister wore blue jeans and a faded chambray shirt. Tomorrow, the entire wedding party would be decked out in western wear, complete with boots, cowboy hats, chaps and spurs. Tanner had left his spurs back at the hotel for the rehearsal, but he'd worn the new boots he'd purchased in Dallas, along with his black felt cowboy hat.

An old-fashioned pump organ was set up in the hayloft and the nesting barn swallows kept swooping down at the organist's head. Her rendition of Mendelssohn's "Wedding March" was punctuated with shrill yelps of terror.

Fortunately, it didn't take long for the minister to run through the vows and position the wedding party in the appropriate places. Tanner's only duty as best man was to hold on to the wedding rings and stand by Cabe—and to pretend it didn't matter to him that he'd lost the only woman he'd given a second glance in over a year.

The minister wiped his perspiring brow with a handkerchief. "At this point, you may kiss the bride."

Tanner's smile froze as he watched Cabe pull Hannah into his arms and rehearse a kiss that they'd obviously practiced many times before.

The kiss went on and on and on.

"Hey, Cabe, save something for the ceremony," Tanner joked, determined never to let Cabe or Hannah see the envy twisting inside of him.

Hannah laughed when Cabe finally released her. "If this is the rehearsal, I can't wait to experience the real thing!"

Cabe grinned. "Maybe we should just have the minister marry us right now so we can proceed straight to the honeymoon."

Hannah's eyes widened. "Oh, Cabe, you're not serious!"

"Why not?" Cabe turned to Tanner. "Do you have the rings?"

Tanner patted his jeans pocket. "They're right here, safe and sound. But you've already reserved the barn and put a down payment on the reception hall. Then there is the caterer to consider, and the band. Both will demand to be paid even if you don't use their services."

"See," Hannah said with a laugh, "at least someone is sensible around here."

Tanner's jaw clenched. *Sensible.* Now he was not only dull and boring, but sensible. How much worse could it get?

Hannah turned to him. "Oh, before I forget, I wanted to tell you that my cousin Jane is coming to the wedding tomorrow. You'll adore her, Tanner, I just know it. She's so sweet—a little quiet though. But she loves to talk about embroidery, so that would be a good icebreaker." Hannah turned back to Cabe. "Jane embroidered ten sets of matching pillowcases for us as a wedding present."

Cabe winced at Tanner over his fiancée's head. "Honey, maybe Tanner already has a date for the wedding."

"Oh," Hannah exclaimed, turning to Tanner. "I never thought of that. Do you?"

"Yes," he improvised, before he found himself shackled to a blind date for the wedding reception. He'd had more than his share of dreary dates lately. He didn't want someone sweet and quiet. He wanted a woman who excited him. A woman who was completely unpredictable. A woman who would agree to attend a wedding with a perfect stranger at a moment's notice.

And now he had less than twenty-four hours to find her.

SHE'D FOUND HIM.

Maddie took a deep, calming breath as she looked around her hotel room, making certain everything was in place. She hadn't been thrilled about the two-hundred-dollar-a-night room charge, although it would definitely be worth it if she could pull this off.

She'd arrived in Texas three days ago and traced Tanner Blackburn to a house in Dallas. It had been surprisingly easy, but then he probably hadn't expected a bounty hunter to locate him through the *Texas Mail-Order Men* magazine, especially since ninety-nine percent of the bounty hunters were men.

A chat with Tanner's next-door neighbor had revealed that Mr. Blackburn was planning a weekend trip to Abilene to attend a wedding. Several phone calls later, Maddie had all the information she needed. Tanner Blackburn had a room reserved for two nights at the Huntington Hotel in Abilene.

She'd tailed him from Dallas. Seen him register at the hotel, then leave again. After registering for her own room and setting everything in place for the takedown, she'd gone back to the lobby for surveillance.

After spending three hours in the lobby pretending to read the newspaper, she'd finally seen him return with a small group of people, half of them heading for the elevators, the other half making a beeline for the bar. Blackburn had joined the group at the bar.

He'd played into her plan perfectly.

Maddie had returned to her hotel room to make certain everything was ready when she brought Blackburn here. She knew she had to play this game carefully. One screwup and she'd lose not only the Kissing Bandit, but her dream to join the family business.

She walked over to the bed, adjusting the pillows. Then she checked once more for anything he might be able to use as a potential weapon. She'd already hidden the glasses, ashtrays, mirrors and other breakables.

Not that she expected him to turn violent. Her extensive study of the Kissing Bandit's methods had taught her that he preferred to use his wiles instead of weapons.

But a girl could never be too careful.

"It's almost time," Maddie said aloud. She'd waited for this moment for so long. Her first takedown. And since she hadn't seen or spoken to her father or brothers in over a week, she didn't have to worry about Tate and Ben interfering this time. She'd taken extra care to make certain they couldn't trace her whereabouts.

The *Texas Mail-Order Men* magazine lay open on the desk. She picked it up and studied the man's picture once more. Blackburn had altered his appearance somewhat, which was only natural when you were a fugitive from justice. She stared at the photograph, a tingle of excitement racing through her veins. Soon she'd be meeting the elusive Kissing Bandit face to face.

Maddie slid the magazine into the desk drawer, then slipped into a pair of high heels, ignoring that her knees were shaking. She checked her makeup in the mirror, applying a last dab of cherry-red lipstick to her mouth. Her plan was definitely risky. Playing the femme fatale had never been her forte. Although she'd attracted her share of men, they always seemed to lose interest in her after the first date. And she couldn't entirely blame her overprotective brothers.

Maddie knew her flaws better than anyone. She was too stubborn, too bossy, too self-reliant. Most men liked to play the hero for a woman. Impress her with his muscles and machismo. They didn't like a woman who knew how to take care of herself. Her own family had taught her that much.

She smoothed her hands over the snug fabric of her red dress, hoping the exorbitant price she'd paid would be worth it. The agency would receive eight thousand dollars if Blackburn was turned over to the court in time. But that time was running out. A bail jumper had to be returned to the custody of the court within one hundred and eighty days of his failure to appear. Otherwise the bail bondsmen had to pay the entire amount of the bond, which in this case was eighty thousand dollars.

The Griffin Bail Enforcement Agency was on the payroll of several Chicago area bail bondsmen, and their reputation for catching elusive felons like the Kissing Bandit was unparalleled in the Chicago area.

Now it was up to Maddie to maintain that reputation. She had just nine days left to bring Blackburn to justice. Adrenaline shot through her veins as she walked toward the door.

The Kissing Bandit was about to be unmasked.

2

TANNER SAT IN THE empty hotel bar, nursing his beer. The wedding party had retired to their rooms, most of them exhausted from the long trip into Abilene. But Tanner was on a mission. Find a woman to take to the wedding tomorrow or learn more than he ever wanted to know about embroidery.

Unfortunately, his hopes for snagging a date were fading fast. He still wore his cowboy hat, since his sister had once informed him that women were attracted to the rugged, outdoorsy type. He might not actually live on a ranch, but he did spend plenty of time outdoors. A former state champion swimmer, Tanner still worked out four evenings a week at the local recreation center. He glanced at the clock, wondering if he'd have more luck impressing the ladies down at the hotel swimming pool.

Surprised to see it was close to midnight, Tanner drained his beer mug. Hannah had suggested he turn in early so he'd be fresh for the wedding tomorrow. But he just wanted to be numb.

"Can I buy you a beer, cowboy?"

He slowly turned around to see a tall, slender brunette. She had big brown eyes and silky nutmeg hair that caressed her bare shoulders. She wore a strapless red sundress that hugged her mouthwatering figure. The three-inch heels on her matching red pumps made her long legs seem endless.

He swallowed hard, then abruptly stood up and motioned to the bar stool beside him. "Only if I can buy you one first."

She sat down, then held out one slender hand. "My name is Giselle, but all my friends call me Gigi."

He opened his mouth, then closed it again. Somehow he guessed a woman named Giselle wouldn't be interested in an estate lawyer. She'd want someone exciting. Impulsive. Someone who lived life on the edge. He could imagine the interest fading from her beautiful eyes as soon as he said, *"Hi, I'm Tanner and I manage the affairs of dead people."*

So why say it?

Tanner straddled his bar stool and spoke before he had time for tedious second thoughts. "My name is Whip. I'm a bull rider."

Her finely winged brows arched in surprise. "Really? I've never met a bull rider before."

Tanner propped his cowboy boot on the rung of her bar stool. "It gets a little rough sometimes."

"I can imagine," she said, obviously impressed.

He tried to remember all the stories his brother Ronnie had told him about the rodeo. Most of them had been highly exaggerated, but entertaining. He signaled the bartender for two beers, mentally weaving a story that would keep her smiling.

It was amazing how easy it was to fall back into the playboy role after all these years.

Gigi crossed her impossibly long legs. "So are you in Abilene to ride bulls?"

"Actually, I'm here for a wedding."

She reached into the bowl of stale popcorn that sat on the bar between them. "I love weddings."

Just the words he wanted to hear. Gigi would be the perfect woman to take as his date, if he could convince her to go with him. *Take it slow, Blackburn. Don't scare her off.*

But Gigi definitely didn't look scared. She leaned toward him, her foot lightly brushing against his ankle.

He watched, mesmerized as she slowly licked the salt from her fingertips. It had been too long since he'd been with a woman. Much too long.

Tanner cleared his throat. "This wedding is a little unusual. I met the bride in a mail-order magazine."

Her eyes widened. "Really?"

"Well, it's a little complicated," he said, realizing he'd given her the wrong impression. Not that he wanted to explain by telling her Hannah had dumped him, especially since he could barely think straight. Either the beer or her subtle, exotic scent had intoxicated him. Maybe both.

"No, I think it's fascinating." She gave him an encouraging smile. "Tell me about the magazine. Did strange women contact you?"

"Day and night," he said, tipping up his hat. He might be stretching the truth just a little, but it was getting easier by the minute. "I'll admit I did it as a lark, but it paid off." *For Cabe, anyway.*

She smiled. "Something tells me you like to live dangerously."

"Whenever possible." His whole body tightened as his gaze fell to her full, sultry mouth. She wasn't anything like Hannah, but there was something about her that pulled at him. Something that triggered a deep, primal urge that made him want to throw her over his shoulder and haul her back to his cave. Or at least his hotel room. He took a deep gulp of beer to cool his blood.

"So tell me about bull riding," she said, reaching for another handful of popcorn.

Tanner spent the next hour making up the wildest stories possible. Fortunately, he'd been to enough rodeos to sound credible. And Gigi's riveted attention and enthusiastic questions encouraged him to keep talking. Three beers later, he'd almost convinced himself that he was one of the best bull riders in Texas. Or at least one of the best at shooting the bull.

"I'm on a hiatus now," Tanner said, rubbing his knee. "Trying to heal up after that last ride."

"Have you ever ridden Diablo?"

"Who?"

She circled one fingertip around the rim of her beer mug. "I saw a special on television once about rodeo bulls, and they said Diablo was known as the meanest one on the rodeo circuit."

"I...uh...no," he said, suddenly wary that he was about to blow his cover.

But she didn't press the point. Instead she gazed up at him. "Your eyes are very blue, aren't they?"

"As blue as the Texas sky," Tanner improvised, emphasizing his Texas drawl for effect. "That's what my mama always said."

His mother, who never permitted any of her three children to call her mama, had never said any such thing. But Mom was in Florida at the moment, so what did it matter?

"Your face is so classic." She reached out her fingers and brushed them lightly across his jaw. "I'd love to do you nude."

He blinked. "Excuse me?"

She laughed. "Did I mention that I'm an artist?"

"No, ma'am," he said, mortified by the blush warming his cheeks. Whip the Bull Rider would never blush.

She reached into her purse and pulled out a small lavender card. "This is my business card. I'm in Abilene for a showing at the Courtyard Gallery."

He took the card from her, noting the New York

City address and the fact that she didn't include her last name on the card, only Giselle.

"Whip, I know this may sound a little forward." She gently laid her hand on his arm, causing his muscles to jerk in response. "But would you mind coming up to my hotel room? I'm just itching to sketch you."

"I never say no to a lady." Especially a lady who wanted to take his clothes off.

"Good." She slid off the bar stool and reached for his hand. "I promise to make it an experience you'll never forget."

His heart pounded in his chest as he followed her to the elevator. When he'd first seen Gigi, all he'd wanted was a date for Cabe's wedding. Now he wanted more.

Much more.

Maybe he should skip his trip to Jamaica and stick around Abilene instead. He couldn't think of a more enjoyable way to spend his vacation than with the sexy and intriguing Giselle.

Standing next to her in the elevator, he closed his eyes, breathing in her unique scent. He'd never been this intrigued by a woman before. He wished he'd foregone that last beer at the bar, wanting all his senses keen and sharp. Somehow he knew this was a night he wouldn't want to forget.

The elevator doors opened and Tanner's pulse kicked up another notch as they headed down a long hallway. Picking up strange women in bars wasn't his usual style.

Judging by the way Gigi's hands were shaking as she tried to insert the plastic key card into the lock of her room, picking up strange men wasn't her style either. She swore softly under her breath when the light on the door lock flashed red instead of green. She tried it again, then a third time.

Tanner deftly took the key card out of her hand, turned it around so the arrow pointed in the right direction, then slid it smoothly into the lock. The light flashed green and he turned the handle to open the door.

"Thank you," she said, a pretty blush suffusing her cheeks. She retrieved the key card from him, then placed one hand on his chest. "Would you mind waiting out here for just a moment? I'd really like to straighten up the room just a bit."

"That's not necessary...." he began, taking a step forward. But she'd already slipped inside and closed the door behind her.

He stared at it, slightly confused. Gigi had seemed a little nervous on the elevator. Was she already having second thoughts?

He mentally kicked himself. Whip the Bull Rider wouldn't have let a woman keep him waiting in the hallway. He'd have carried her over the threshold and showed her his real talents. Just when he was about to give up hope, she opened the door again.

He strode inside without a word, then pulled her into his arms. A small gasp escaped her mouth right before he kissed her. She tasted of butter and salt and beer. And something else. Something uniquely Gigi that made him pull her even closer and deepen the kiss.

She moaned low in her throat and circled her arms around his neck. Without breaking the kiss, he kicked the hotel door shut behind him.

The kiss smoldered between them, so thrilling and hot that he never wanted it to end. At last he lifted his head, tantalized by the raw desire he saw gleaming in her brown eyes. "You're incredible, Gigi."

She swallowed, then took a deep, shuddering breath. "You're not exactly what I expected."

He grinned. "Good."

She reached up and undid the top button of his shirt. "Whip, I have a confession to make."

He sucked in his breath as her fingers slid down to the second button. "A confession?"

"I really did want to sketch you, but now..."

She stood so close to him that he could smell the sweet raspberry fragrance of her hair. Her fingers slowly teased each button out of its buttonhole. At last, his shirt gaped open and her warm breath caressed his bare chest.

"Now...what?" he asked huskily. He liked the way her sundress outlined the generous curves of her body. Liked the way she kept licking her lips, as if savoring the kiss they had just shared.

She tugged his shirttails out of his jeans. "Now I want to do so much more."

His gaze fell on the king-size bed that dominated the entire room. "So do I."

Without another word, she turned around and opened the hotel room door, placing the Do Not Disturb sign on the exterior door handle. Then she closed it again and flipped the lock.

He moved toward her, but she smiled and held up one hand. "Don't move. Not yet. I want to look at you."

She walked slowly toward him, her gaze lingering on his chest, then gliding downward. His body reacted as if she was actually touching him and it took all his willpower not to pull her into his arms.

"You're so big." Her hands slid slowly up his chest. "So tall and strong."

He closed his eyes with a low groan of pleasure at her touch. But despite the desire pounding in his veins, he willed himself not to move. He let her set the pace, enjoying every moment of this exquisite torture.

Her hands smoothed over his skin and he opened his eyes when she touched the small scar below his left nipple.

"Did this happen while you were bull riding?"

She slowly slid her finger back and forth over the pale pink scar.

His nipple tightened at the feathery sensation. He nodded, not wanting to ruin the moment by telling her the real story. Somehow he didn't think she'd be impressed that he'd tripped on a staircase in high school and been pierced by the metal math compass in his shirt pocket.

Her hands hungrily caressed his ribs, her fingers running through his chest hair, then over his shoulders as she pushed his shirt halfway down his arms.

She was so close, he couldn't breathe right. Couldn't think straight. His body tightened as the front of her dress brushed against his bare chest. He could feel her firm breasts through the thin fabric. More than ever, he wanted to hold her, kiss her senseless. But his arms were now pinioned by his shirt. It was an odd sensation, being at her mercy, that he found strangely erotic.

"What do you want?" she breathed, slowly guiding him backward toward the bed.

He wanted so many wonderful things. Things only Gigi could give him. "You," he said, lowering his head to nuzzle the tender skin behind her ear.

She leaned into him, causing him to fall back onto the bed. A bolt of pain shot up his arms, still trapped behind his back. But he quickly forgot about the discomfort as Gigi followed him onto the bed, straddling his waist.

She leaned down until her lips were only a hairs-breadth away from his mouth. "I knew I wanted you as soon as I saw you."

"Me, too," he murmured, then tipped his head up just far enough to kiss her. He moaned as his tongue slipped inside her mouth. The sweet taste of her, combined with the incredible sensation of her bare legs wrapped snugly around his waist, was almost more than he could bear.

Somewhere in his frazzled mind, he knew he should confess, too. Tell her he wasn't really Whip the Bull Rider. And that he'd never met a woman like her before.

But now certainly wasn't the time. Not when she was so warm and soft and inviting. Her tongue arched into his mouth at the same time her hands flexed against his shoulders. She deepened the kiss, putting so much enthusiasm into it that his head fell back onto the pillow.

Tanner lay there, completely at her mercy, unable to touch her with anything but his mouth. It heightened every sensation. He could smell the soapy scent of the freshly laundered pillowcase and feel every inch of her warm body pressed against his own. One silky tendril of her hair teased his left ear.

He arched his hips upward, welcoming the delicious friction of her body against his aroused flesh. Despite the long dry spell in his love life, he could never remember reacting to a woman like this before.

At last she broke the kiss and rose to a sitting position, her soft, silky thighs cradling his hips. The hem of the sundress was pushed up past her knees. Her breathing was fast and heavy.

"I need to touch you," he said huskily.

A high flush stained her creamy cheeks. "Turn over."

He readily obliged, anxious to have her rip his shirt off and free his arms. Then he could finally touch her. Undress her. Lose himself in her.

But instead of yanking his shirt off, she straddled his backside. Then she leaned down, her soft, buttery breath curling inside of his ear. "Do you like to play games, Whip?"

Before he could reply, she slid her hand under the pillow and pulled out something pink. It took a moment before he realized they were handcuffs.

Very unusual handcuffs.

"Uh...what exactly do you have in mind?" he asked, as she dangled the pink ménage à trois cuffs in front of his face. There were three individual cuffs connected by a Y-shaped, silk-covered chain.

"You'll see," she teased, then slapped one of the three cuffs onto his right wrist. He barely had time to blink before she shackled his left wrist as well.

He lay there, trying to decide exactly what Whip the Bull Rider would do in this situation. But desire and anticipation had clouded his brain. He tried to turn over, but her weight kept him firmly anchored to the mattress.

Tanner tugged on his wrists, but the handcuffs held tight. "Uh...Gigi?"

"Yes?"

"This is a little uncomfortable."

She rolled off of him. "Let me see what I can do."

He frowned in confusion as she bent his right leg at the knee and slipped off his cowboy boot. Then he heard another click and realized too late that she'd locked the third empty cuff around his ankle.

He lay there hog-tied and completely helpless.

Where had he ever gotten the idiotic idea that picking up a strange woman in a bar would be fun? Of course, it had been fun when she'd been taking his shirt off. And it had been beyond fun when she'd kissed him.

Somehow, somewhere, they'd taken a wrong turn. He arched his head up far enough to see her smiling at him.

Then she gave him a saucy wink. "Gotcha, cowboy."

3

"WHAT THE HELL IS GOING on here?"

Maddie tensed as the Kissing Bandit yanked hard on the handcuffs, but they held tight. Beneath all that pink silk was solid core steel. "You need to calm down."

He took a deep breath, his face pressed halfway into the pillow. "Look, Gigi, I don't think it's going to work out between us after all."

She rolled her eyes. The man was gorgeous, but completely clueless. "Haven't you figured it out yet? I'm not Gigi. My name is Maddie Griffin and I'm from the Griffin Bail Enforcement Agency in Chicago."

He stopped moving. "What?"

"You heard me, cowboy. You're all mine." She took a deep breath, still a little shaky from her first takedown. It had all gone according to plan. Sort of. She hadn't actually intended to let him kiss her, or to kiss him back. But that didn't matter now.

She had him exactly where she wanted him.

"You're a bounty hunter?" he said at last, his blue eyes wide with disbelief.

"That's right." She stood beside the bed, waiting for him to accept the situation. He'd soon tire of fighting the handcuffs.

"Well, I hate to break it to you, but you've got the wrong man. My name isn't really Whip. I made that up...."

"I know," she interjected. "You're the Kissing Bandit."

"Who?"

"The Kissing Bandit." She reached down, unable to resist brushing a lock of hair out of his eyes. "I realize Tanner Blackburn is your alias du jour, but even if the name changes, the crime stays the same. You've been scamming women for the past seven years, but your luck just ran out. I'm taking you in."

"This is ridiculous." He bucked once, his breathing heavy. "I *am* Tanner Blackburn and I'm an attorney from Dallas. I should warn you that forcibly holding someone against their will is a felony in this state."

She arched a brow. "A lawyer? I thought you were a bull rider."

He clenched his jaw. "I made that up."

"Just like you made up the name Whip?"

"Yes."

She folded her arms across her chest. "Somehow that doesn't sound like something an innocent man would do."

"I had my reasons," he said between clenched teeth.

"Now *that* I believe." She slipped off her high heels, relishing the feel of the plush carpet against the soles of her feet. "Advertising your services in the *Texas Mail-Order Men* magazine is the standard m.o. for the Kissing Bandit. So is preying on helpless, vulnerable women."

"Helpless?" He struggled to lift his head off the pillow. "I'd hardly call you helpless. Crazy, yes. Helpless, no."

She smiled. "You're just mad because I gave you a taste of your own medicine."

He stopped moving and stared up at her. "Are you telling me this was all a ploy? The beers at the bar. The invitation to your hotel room. The kiss."

She forced herself to meet his gaze, wishing she could forget about that kiss. It definitely hadn't been part of her plan. She was only supposed to sketch him. But he'd caught her off guard when he'd marched into her hotel room and kissed her. So she'd improvised. Then, after she'd peeled his shirt over his shoulders to secure his arms, she hadn't been able to resist kissing him again.

Now Maddie just wished she could forget the way her body had responded to him. It wasn't just embarrassing, it was unprofessional. For one brief, insane, electrifying moment she had forgotten the real reason she'd brought him up to her hotel room.

"Tell me," he demanded, obviously irritated by her silence, "do you really have a showing at an art gallery? Are you even from New York? Or were you just playing games with me?"

She tipped up her chin. "What do you think?"

His shoulders sagged. "I think I'm an idiot."

"Don't take it so hard. Your luck couldn't hold out forever."

He closed his eyes. "This is beyond crazy. I am not the Kissing Bandit. I'm an estate lawyer."

"Is that one of your new scams? I imagine there is quite a profit in seducing wealthy widows."

"It's not a scam, it's the truth. I'm with the law firm of Collins and Cooksey. The only reason I made up Whip the Bull Rider was to impress you."

"I'm definitely impressed with your creative abilities—" she sat on the edge of the bed "—although I do think it's a little disgusting that you're in a bar trying to pick up women the night before your wedding."

"My wedding?" His brow furrowed. "Where did you get a crazy idea like that?"

"From you. Down at the bar you told me that you'd met the bride through the *Texas Mail-Order Men* magazine. I believe your exact words were—*It paid off*."

He shook his head. "No, you've got it all wrong. I tried to tell you that before, but you distracted me."

"Oh, sure. Blame the victim."

"Victim." He snorted. "I'm the one whose leg is growing numb. Now please unlock these cuffs."

Maddie could see his discomfort, but she steeled herself against the appeal in his blue eyes. A bounty hunter couldn't risk feeling sorry for her fugitives or allow herself to make concessions. Besides, the man deserved a little discomfort after all the pain he'd caused her father—not to mention all the women whose hearts he'd broken.

"I'll unlock them when we get to Chicago."

His eyes widened. "Chicago?"

She nodded. "That's where we're headed as soon as the sun comes up tomorrow. I've been tracking you for the past three days and I'm a little behind schedule."

"I'm not going anywhere with you." He lunged upward, but only succeeded in rolling off the bed. He hit the carpet with a loud grunt.

She kneeled down on the floor beside him. "It won't do you any good to try to escape."

"Escape?" he sputtered, wincing as he rolled onto his side. "Sorry to disappoint you, but at the moment I'm just hoping I didn't break any bones."

Her sympathy overcame her better judgment. She pulled a small key from the pocket of her sundress and unlocked the cuff around his ankle. He slowly straightened his right leg, wincing at the movement. Maddie didn't waste any time securing the empty cuff around the metal leg of the bed frame.

"There," she said, helping him up to a sitting position, his arms still cuffed behind his back. "That's better."

"No, that's not better. I demand that you release me immediately!" He yanked hard on his chains.

"Sorry, Whip. No can do."

"The name is Tanner."

"This week, anyway." She sat down in a chair across from him.

A muscle twitched in his jaw. "Face it, lady, you nabbed the wrong man."

She sighed. "It's not going to work."

"My name is Tanner Blackburn," he insisted.

"And you're a lawyer."

"That's right."

"A successful lawyer?"

He nodded. "As a matter of fact, I'm on the fast track to making partner."

"Impressive." She leaned forward. "So tell me something. Why would a handsome, successful lawyer advertise himself in the *Texas Mail-Order Men* magazine?"

He met her gaze and her stomach fluttered at the indefinable emotion swirling in his blue eyes. "It's a long story."

"That's all right, Whip...I mean, Tanner." She settled back in her chair. "It's not like you're going anywhere."

She forced herself to remain calm as he worked

himself into a fury, yanking on the chains hard enough to make the bed vibrate. He was much brawnier than she'd expected. His shoulders were wide and his chest unbelievably broad. He'd obviously been working out since that last mug shot had been taken.

Her mouth went dry when she remembered the way his chest muscles had rippled beneath her touch. How the bulge of his biceps had helped snag his shirtsleeves behind him, making it almost impossible for him to move his arms.

She'd known the Kissing Bandit had charmed women all over the country, but she'd never really understood his magnetic power...until tonight.

The man had a boyish appeal that was almost irresistible. Especially when it was combined with those incredible blue eyes, that solid, square jaw, and a smile that melted something deep inside of her.

Not to mention that kiss.

She closed her eyes, attempting to block out the memory, and failing. Her body had betrayed her, and it still thrummed from the aftereffects of his kiss. She kept telling herself the only reason she'd kissed him was to distract him when she brought out the handcuffs.

But it wasn't true. Worse, it had almost backfired on her. No wonder so many women had signed over their bank accounts and their common sense to this man.

"Am I boring you?" he asked archly.

Her eyes flew open. "Did you say something?"

His nostrils flared. "I was telling you the reason my picture was in that stupid magazine."

She tucked her legs underneath her. "I can't wait to hear it."

He shifted uncomfortably on the floor. "Then I'll say it again. It was a gift."

She arched a brow, surprised that a man as cunning as the Kissing Bandit couldn't come up with something more clever. "You consider yourself a gift to women?"

"No. It was a gift to my little sister." He sagged against the bed, obviously exhausted from his struggle against the handcuffs. "For some ridiculous reason, she thought I didn't have enough romance in my life. So she filled out the application and told me the only thing she wanted for her high school graduation present was my picture in the *Texas Mail-Order Men* magazine."

As far as Maddie knew, the Kissing Bandit didn't have a little sister. But she decided to play along anyway. "And you agreed?"

"Not at first," he replied. "But Lauren is nothing if not persistent. She told me she couldn't enjoy herself at college if I was all alone in Dallas."

Maddie had to give him credit. He was good. Very good.

Especially the way his voice softened when he

spoke his sister's name. He was a master of deception, which was probably the reason he'd avoided capture for so long.

"So you advertised yourself in the magazine hoping to find true love?"

"Something like that." A muscle flexed in his jaw. "Look, the real reason is that it made my sister happy. She's had a tough time these last few years, but she pulled herself together and graduated from high school with honors. She even qualified for a college scholarship. So when she asked me to put my picture in the *Texas Mail-Order Men* magazine, I did it. Hell, I would have walked across hot coals if she'd asked me to. And considering the way this evening is turning out, that might have been more fun."

Maddie studied him, wondering how long it took him to create these cockamamie stories. At least this one was more plausible than the wild rodeo adventures he'd spun down at the bar. Did he improvise on the spur of the moment or spend hours concocting heart-wrenching tales to make women fall in love with him?

He certainly *seemed* like the perfect catch. Not only was he sinfully handsome, but he treated his little sister like a princess. No doubt leaving the impression that he'd treat the love of his life even better.

Too bad it was all make-believe.

"Do you adopt orphaned puppies and help little old ladies across the street, too?" she asked, tired of playing games. The rush of adrenaline from the take-down was finally beginning to wear off.

He narrowed his eyes. "What's that supposed to mean?"

"Just that I'm smart enough not to believe a word that comes out of your mouth."

"It happens to be the truth."

"Okay," she said, happy to call his bluff. "Give me your sister's phone number and I'll call her up to verify your story."

"You can't call her," he retorted, anger sparking in his blue eyes. "Lauren went camping with friends this weekend. She won't be home until Sunday."

"That's convenient."

"It's the damn truth!"

"Your bedtime stories are making me sleepy." She got up and switched off the light, blanketing the room in darkness. "Good night, Whip."

Tension crackled in the air as she walked over to the bed and pulled back the covers. But it wasn't until her head hit the pillow that he finally spoke.

"You expect me to sleep here on the floor like this?" He tugged on the handcuffs, shaking the bed slightly.

"Well, you're certainly not sleeping with me," Maddie replied, thankful for the darkness that covered her blush. Because, despite her best efforts, she couldn't seem to forget that interlude on the bed right before she'd handcuffed him. The Kissing Bandit might be one of the world's best con men, but she hadn't been acting.

Still, what did it matter now? She'd done it. She'd brought down the Kissing Bandit. Satisfaction warmed her as she imagined the expression on her father's face when she brought Blackburn in. Her brothers would be dumbfounded, and jealous as hell.

She could hardly wait.

4

TANNER AWOKE SLOWLY THE next morning, wincing at the piercing ache in his shoulders. It took him a moment to remember why he was lying on the floor. And why both of his hands were numb.

Maddie.

That brown-eyed vixen had lured him right into her trap. And he'd drooled over her all the way there. He closed his eyes, thoroughly disgusted with himself. This was certainly not the way he intended to start his well-earned vacation.

He rolled to one side, then levered himself up to a sitting position. His stiff muscles screamed in protest. He'd talked himself hoarse last night trying to convince her she'd made a big mistake. But Maddie Griffin refused to listen to reason. She was the most stubborn woman he'd ever met.

Leaning his head back against the mattress, he heard the shower running in the bathroom. She'd obviously been serious about leaving at the crack of dawn. Closing his eyes, he wondered how the hell he'd gotten into this situation, and more importantly, how he was going to get out of it.

A few minutes later, the shower turned off and he could hear the squeak of the shower door as it opened. It was too easy to imagine Maddie standing naked only a few feet away from him, tiny droplets of water streaming over her delectable body. If he wasn't handcuffed to the bed, he'd be half tempted to walk in there and join her. Finish what they had started last night.

Last night. The wedding rehearsal. *Oh, hell.*

"Maddie!" He craned his neck toward the bathroom door. "Get out here right now!"

A moment later, the door opened and she stuck out her wet head, a towel hanging in front of her. "Is there a problem?"

"Damn right there's a problem. I'm supposed to be in a wedding this afternoon. You've got to let me out of here."

She rolled her eyes. "Right. I'm going to release you so you can go marry some poor, unsuspecting woman and steal her blind. Give me a break."

"I'm the best man," he began, right before she slammed the bathroom door shut.

All right. It was obvious Maddie wouldn't listen to reason. Or rather, wouldn't listen to *him*. Maybe she just needed someone else to convince her. He eyed the telephone on the nightstand. If he could reach it, then all he had to do was dial up Cabe's room and this entire mess could finally be straightened out.

He stretched out to his full length, pulling the

chain attached to the bedpost taut as he arched his foot toward the nightstand. Gritting his teeth, he looped his big toe around the telephone cord coiled onto the carpet. It caught, then slipped away. He tried it a second time, then a third.

Sweat beaded his brow as he took a deep breath and attempted it a fourth time. When the cord caught on his toe, he yanked hard and the telephone on the nightstand jerked.

"Yes!" With the cord closer now, Tanner used his foot to painstakingly pull it towards him. The telephone finally slid off the nightstand, landing on the thick beige carpet with a loud ding.

He froze, hoping Maddie wouldn't rush out here at the noise. But the sound of a blow-dryer made him breathe a sigh of relief. She obviously hadn't heard a thing. Still, he knew he didn't have time to waste.

Dragging the telephone towards him inch by excruciating inch, Tanner finally got it close enough so he could bend down and flip the receiver off with his chin. With his arms still pinioned behind his back, he couldn't dial the push-button phone with his fingers. So he improvised with his tongue instead, using the tip of it to depress the zero button on the dial pad. Then he laid his head on the floor, his ear pressed close to the receiver.

"This is the hotel operator," a crisp voice said over the line. "How may I direct your call?"

Exhilaration at his success flowed through his veins. "Cabe White's room," he said in a low voice.

"One moment, please."

His gut tightened as he heard the blow-dryer shut off. She couldn't come out now, not when he was so close.

The operator came back on the line. "My pleasure to connect you."

Tanner closed his eyes as he heard the sweet sound of ringing in his ear. Then a second ring. Then a third. "C'mon, Cabe. Answer the phone!"

After the seventh ring, a low, gravelly voice sounded over the line. "Yeah?"

"Cabe? Is that you?"

"Yeah."

"This is Tanner. I'm in big trouble."

"Yeah."

"Are you awake?" he asked in a frustrated whisper.

"Yeah."

"Okay, then listen. Some crazy woman lured me up to her hotel room last night and locked me in kinky handcuffs."

"Yeah."

"Cabe, wake up, damn it! Did you hear a word I said?"

"Some crazy woman," Cabe mumbled. "Handcuffs."

"That's right. She claims she's a bounty hunter

and refuses to let me go. You've got to get me out of here." Tanner paused. "Cabe?"

A snore reverberated over the line.

"Oh, hell," Tanner muttered, then used his chin to cut the connection. When a dial tone sounded, he stabbed the zero button with his tongue again.

"This is the operator. How may I direct your call?"

"Give me Hannah Cavanaugh's room, please." Tanner knew he only had a few minutes left, if that much, before Maddie emerged from the bathroom. He needed to make every second count.

Hannah picked up on the first ring. "Hello."

"This is Tanner. I'm in big trouble."

"You lost the wedding rings!"

"No, I didn't lose the rings. They're still in my pocket." He took a deep breath, trying hard to keep his voice down. "A woman picked me up in the bar last night...."

"Why are you whispering?"

"Just listen," he interjected. "You've got to get me out of here."

"Out of where?"

"Her hotel room. She won't let me go."

Hannah hesitated. "Tanner, have you been drinking?"

"Just listen to me...."

The bathroom door opened and Maddie stepped into the room. "What's going on?" Then she saw the telephone and her mouth thinned. "Very cute."

She reached down and yanked the cord out of the receiver. "Hotel calls are very expensive."

"You didn't have to do that," he said between clenched teeth.

She looked from him to the telephone. "You're more resourceful than I thought. I'll need to keep a better eye on you until we reach Chicago."

"I'm not going anywhere with you, lady." It didn't help his mood any that she looked wonderful. She wore another sundress, pink this time. It gave her dewy skin a rosy glow. Her brown eyes sparkled and her lips looked even more kissable than they had last night.

"Are you sure about that?"

"Positive."

She smiled. "I think I know a way to change your mind."

TANNER SAT IN SULLEN silence as Maddie retrieved a bulky black bag from the closet. A huge yellow smiley face adorned one side.

"It's time for a little show-and-tell."

"I'm not in the mood," he muttered.

She smiled. "Fortunately, you're a captive audience." She pulled a chair in front of him and sat down. Then she reached into the bag and pulled out a black object that was curved at the top and about six inches in length.

"Do you know what this is?" she asked, holding it up for him to see.

"A can opener?"

"Not even close. It's a stun gun. I use it on fugitives who decide they don't want to cooperate. The side effects are a little...unpleasant."

Unpleasant? Tanner had heard what a stun gun could do to a person. Unpleasant was definitely an understatement.

"I also have pepper spray," she said, pulling out the next tool of her trade. "My weapon of choice in most circumstances, since it's user friendly."

He stared at her, unable to believe this was the same woman who had almost seduced him last night. She looked the same, but she talked like a cross-dressing Rambo.

She dug through the bag. "And leg shackles and a standard pair of handcuffs."

"Can I make a trade? Pink really isn't my color."

She looked up at him. "At least they don't chafe."

He shook his head, unable to believe a woman toting a stun gun would care whether his wrists chafed. But then she *had* wiggled a pillow under his head last night when she'd thought he was asleep. And covered him with a blanket. So maybe she wasn't as tough as she liked to pretend.

Or as confident.

Tanner considered that possibility. Despite her bag of mercenary tricks, Maddie still had to find a way to walk him through the hotel lobby and out into the parking lot. Once he was out of this hotel room and surrounded by people, surely he could find some way to gain his freedom.

She methodically replaced all the weapons into the bag. Everything except the pepper spray. Then she stood up. "Time to hit the road, cowboy."

He glanced at the digital clock on the nightstand. It wasn't even seven o'clock yet. No doubt the lobby would still be empty this early. He needed to figure out some way to delay her for at least an hour. Besides, the more he could screw up her schedule, the better his chances of escaping her gorgeous clutches.

Tanner patiently waited while she unlocked the cuff around the bedpost, then helped him to his feet. His legs felt wobbly and his shoulders sore from sleeping with his arms cinched behind his back all night. Little did she know he couldn't attempt an escape right now even if she didn't have the pepper spray aimed at his face.

His stomach growled, breaking the silence between them.

A reluctant smile rose to Maddie's lips. "We'll pick up something for breakfast on our way out of Abilene."

"Wait," he said, as she tugged on his arm. "I...need to use the bathroom."

Her smile turned to a frown as she glanced up at him. "Are you sure?"

He grimaced. "Positive. I did have quite a few beers last night, remember?"

She sighed. "Okay. But no tricks."

Tanner crossed his fingers behind his back. "No tricks."

She led him inside the bathroom, the air still steamy from her shower. He slipped on the wet tile floor and stumbled against her, unable to catch himself with his hands cuffed behind his back.

Maddie reached out to steady him, her arms wrapping around his waist. Tanner's cheek grazed her chin as he fell against her. She backed up to the sink with his full weight pressed against her, his head nestled in the crook of her shoulder.

His mouth pressed against the curve of her neck. The creamy, tender skin was almost too tempting to resist.

"Are you all right?" she asked, sounding slightly breathless.

He closed his eyes, wishing he'd get over this irrational fascination with her. He should not be having erotic fantasies about a woman who just moments ago had threatened to electrocute him with a stun gun.

With a force of effort, he lifted his head. "I'm fine."

"Good." She gazed up into his eyes, a rosy flush in her cheeks.

He was starting to suspect that, despite all her

tough talk, she wasn't immune to him either. A fact he might be able to use to his advantage.

She turned away, hastily hooking the third empty link on the ménage à trois handcuffs to the metal towel bar on the wall. "There. The bathroom is small enough you should be able to reach...everything you need."

She headed toward the door. "Call me when you're ready."

"Wait a minute."

She turned around. "What?"

He lifted his shoulders to indicate his cuffed hands. "I need your help."

She took a step closer to him. "What exactly do you want me to do?"

"Unzip my pants."

He watched her gaze drift downward and her eyes widen at the obvious bulge of his zipper. She swallowed convulsively as she looked back up at him, a hot blush now burning in her cheeks. "I suppose I could uncuff one of your hands."

"I'm completely at your mercy."

She turned him around, a little more roughly than necessary in his opinion, which only confirmed his suspicion that she'd felt the same sparks arcing between them. He smiled as she fumbled with the handcuff key.

At last, he heard a click and his right hand was free.

He flexed his fingers, trying to assuage the tingling sensation.

"There." She backed away from him. "You're all set."

He rubbed his free hand over the thick stubble on his jaw, wondering if she'd consent to lending him a razor. Probably not.

"You've got ten minutes," she said from the bathroom doorway. "Then I'm coming in after you."

5

MADDIE CLOSED THE bathroom door behind her, then took a deep, calming breath. Her heart raced in her chest and she felt a little lightheaded. Somehow, this particular fugitive apprehension wasn't going at all as she'd planned.

Unzip my pants. She still couldn't believe the nerve of that man. His ego was as big as...the rest of his body. She walked to the bed, still shaken by their collision in the bathroom, and hating the way she reacted to him. Especially when she'd seen the smug satisfaction in his eyes.

"Get a grip," she muttered to herself. "You're the one in control here."

Only she didn't feel in control. Blackburn made her feel giddy and nervous and self-conscious. His blue eyes followed her everywhere. And he kept looking at her mouth. As if he remembered that kiss between them as vividly as she did.

What if she couldn't bring him in? He was already playing mind games with her. Trying to make her doubt herself. Maddie mentally kicked herself for letting him see the effect he had on her. Since his indignant innocent act hadn't worked on her, he was obviously trying another tactic.

Unfortunately, it was working.

But she couldn't let him win. She simply had to be strong enough and smart enough to beat him at his own game. Squaring her shoulders, she reached for the telephone and dialed her father's home number.

"Griffin, here," her father answered, fully alert even at this early hour.

"Hi, Dad. It's me."

"Maddie? Where the hell are you?"

She twisted the phone cord around her fingers. "I'm out of town."

"So why didn't you bother to tell me you were leaving? I've been worried sick about you. No one has seen or heard from you for the past week. Your brothers have been out combing the city."

"I didn't mean to make you worry."

"Don't get me wrong," Gus said, calmer now. "I'm glad you're taking some time for yourself. A little vacation will be good for you."

"I'm not on a vacation, Dad." She took a deep breath. "I'm on a case."

An ominous silence crackled over the line.

"You're what?" Gus said at last, his voice tight.

"I'm on a case. In fact, I've already apprehended the fugitive and we're on our way back to Chicago."

"This is no time for jokes, Maddie."

"I'm not joking. I've been tailing the guy for the

past couple of days, waiting for just the right opportunity. The takedown happened last night. And it was perfect." Okay, so maybe she was exaggerating just a little. But her father didn't need to know every little detail.

"Madeline Mae Griffin, you turn the fugitive over to the local authorities, then get your butt back here. Pronto. I mean it!"

She tried not to take offense at his lack of confidence in her, but it stung anyway. If he knew she had none other than the Kissing Bandit in her hotel room, he'd sing a different tune. "I'll be home in a few days, Dad. And I'll have a big surprise for you."

"Where are you? Let me send the boys there...."

"No, Dad," she interjected, "I'm bringing this one in all on my own."

"Madeline...."

She hung up the receiver before he started yelling. It wouldn't do her father any good to lose his temper and raise his blood pressure, especially when she didn't have any intention of changing her mind.

She glanced at the bathroom door. Transporting Blackburn from the hotel room to her car might be a little tricky. No doubt he had some slick scheme ready and was just waiting for a chance to make a run for it.

So she had to come up with a scheme of her own.

TANNER LEANED AGAINST the wall, attempting to pick the lock on the handcuffs with a stray bobby pin he'd found in Maddie's makeup bag. To his chagrin, the towel bar hadn't budged when he'd tried to pry it off the wall.

Twisting the bobby pin in the lock, he briefly wondered where she'd ever found these outrageous pink silk ménage à trois cuffs. And if she ever used them for something besides apprehending fugitives.

As he fished for a better angle in the lock, the bobby pin snapped in two. "Damn."

Tanner sighed, then looked around the tiny, windowless bathroom, debating his options. Even if he did manage to free himself from the handcuffs, he'd still have to face Calamity Maddie waiting for him just outside the door.

She'd been smart enough not to leave any possible weapons within his reach. Not that he could hurt a woman anyway, even a woman who had seduced him into captivity.

But that didn't mean he couldn't inconvenience her as much as possible. Screw up her precious schedule. He shrugged out of his shirt, still unbuttoned from last night's encounter. When it caught on the cuff around his left wrist, he ripped it and tossed it on the floor. Then he awkwardly stripped off his jeans.

"Hey, what's going on in there?" Maddie called through the door.

"Nothing," he said, stepping out of his boxer shorts.

"You've had more than enough time," she shouted. "I'm coming in."

"Okay," he said, as the door cracked open. "But I'm naked."

The door slammed closed again. "Why are you naked?"

He smiled at the frustration in her voice. "Because I've got this strange habit of taking my clothes off before I shower." He turned on the shower tap, adjusting the temperature as steam filled the air.

She shouted something else through the door, but he couldn't decipher it over the rush of water. Whistling, Tanner stepped under the hot spray. Maddie and her precious timetable could wait. He intended to take his sweet time, and drive her crazy in the process, he hoped. The more frustrated she became, the better his chances of getting away.

He stood in the shower stall with the opaque shower door gaped open just far enough to allow room for his outstretched left arm, which was still cuffed to the towel bar. He used Maddie's raspberry shampoo to wash his hair, stirring up memories of last night when she'd been close enough for him to inhale her delicate, enticing scent.

Thirty minutes later, he turned off the tap, thoroughly refreshed and much more optimistic. Maddie might have tricked him into these handcuffs, but she was no match for him, even with that unsettling arsenal of weapons in her little black bag. He'd battled wits with some of the best lawyers in the business.

All he had to do was wait for the right opportunity to make a break for it.

Stepping out of the shower stall, he grabbed a fluffy white towel off the rack. He vigorously dried himself, shivering slightly from the cold air blasting out of the ceiling vent. Then he reached for his clothes.

And came up empty.

His clothes weren't on the floor, or anywhere else in the bathroom.

"All done now?" Maddie called sweetly through the door.

He clenched his jaw, realizing she must have snuck in here while he was in the shower. "Where the hell are my clothes?"

"Are you decent? I have a surprise for you."

He wrapped the towel around his waist. "Yes. But I've had about all the surprises I can take for a while."

The door swung open and Maddie took one step inside the bathroom, still too far away for him to reach. She held a paper bag in one hand and the stun gun in the other. Her gaze took a lingering journey over his body from head to toe. "You do clean up nice."

"You can give me my clothes now."

"First things first." She set down the paper sack, then walked cautiously toward the towel rack, the stun gun at the ready.

Tanner tensed, knowing she was close enough to tackle. Of course, the chances were good that she'd zap him with the stun gun as soon as he made a move. Not liking the odds, he decided to wait for an opportunity to catch her off guard.

Maddie picked up the empty cuff dangling between his shackled wrist and the towel rack, then slapped it around his free wrist.

"Thank you," he said sincerely.

She glanced up at him. "For what?"

"For not cuffing my hands behind my back. It's much more comfortable this way. Of course, it would be even better if you just unlocked them altogether."

"I will," she promised, reaching for the paper sack. "As soon as we reach Chicago."

He decided not to tell her he wouldn't be going with her to Chicago. In fact, he intended to ditch her before they even left the hotel. As soon as they hit the lobby, he'd make a run for it.

"I hope you like yellow."

He stared at the bundle of voluminous yellow plastic she pulled out of the sack. "What is that?"

"Your new outfit."

She reached up and dropped it over his head, adjusting the neck hole as the rain poncho billowed around him, just reaching his knees. There were no armholes and the length effectively concealed both his nakedness and his cuffed hands. "I'm glad they had an extra-tall size in the hotel gift shop."

An uneasy feeling stirred in the pit of his stomach. "Where are the rest of my clothes?"

"In the car. If you're a good boy, I'll let you put on your new boxer shorts as soon as we get there, along with the rest of your clothes."

So his bounty hunter wanted to make sure he had on clean underwear. Tanner was too outraged to be grateful. He took a step toward her, causing the towel wrapped around his waist to loosen, then fall to the floor. Now he was completely naked underneath the poncho. No way could he walk through the hotel lobby wearing this stupid yellow plastic poncho and nothing else. "I'm not going."

She held up the stun gun. "Yes, you are."

He ground his teeth together. His instincts told him that Maddie Griffin didn't have a violent bone in her body. That she was bluffing. But then, his instincts hadn't been too accurate lately or he wouldn't be in this position.

Did he dare call her bluff?

She unlocked the handcuff from the towel rack and led him out of the bathroom. "I will let you wear your cowboy boots."

"How generous of you." Tanner frantically rethought his plan as she helped him on with his boots, then led him out of the hotel room and down the long hallway.

She glanced up at him as they waited in front of the elevator. "I think I should warn you that I called the front desk about ten minutes ago and told them a naked man wearing nothing but pink handcuffs and cowboy boots just tried to attack me by the ice machine."

He stared at her in disbelief. The woman was a complete lunatic.

"So it's up to you, Tanner. You can come to Chicago with me, or take your chances with the good old boys in the Abilene Police Department. Somehow I'd guess they don't take kindly to kinky sex maniacs."

He clenched his jaw. So much for his escape plan. If Collins and Cooksey ever got whiff of a story like that, his chances of making partner would be down the toilet. Hell, it might even ruin his career. "You are some piece of work, lady."

"Thank you." She dropped the stun gun back into her bag as soon as the elevator door slid open.

"I didn't mean it as a compliment." He strode in ahead of her, more frustrated than ever.

Two middle-aged cowboys stood inside the elevator car, both smirking at Tanner in his rain poncho. No doubt it was clear and sunny outside, making him look like an idiot. At least they didn't know what he looked like *under* the rain poncho.

"You're going to pay for this, my sweet Gigi," he vowed under his breath. "You're definitely going to pay."

6

Gus Griffin paced across his office, torn between worrying about his little girl and wishing she was still little enough to bend over his knee. Not that he'd ever actually spanked her. Somehow Maddie had always talked her way out of trouble. But this was different. She was in completely over her pretty head. If he didn't find her fast, he might lose her forever.

He rubbed one hand over his unshaven jaw, realizing he'd never been this scared before. Except once. Fifteen years ago Maddie had balked at his plan to send her to one of the most prestigious boarding schools in the country. She'd run away from home and stayed hidden for two days. When he finally found her, he'd had to drag her kicking and screaming to the airport and pretend her pleas and tears didn't affect him.

Gus Griffin had only cried two times in his life. At his wife's funeral and at the airport the day Maddie had flown to Boston.

Now she was gone again, and he felt just as helpless. His daughter might be classroom smart, but she was naive in the ways of the world. Just the thought of her in the slimy clutches of some two-bit hood made his throat grow tight and his fists clench.

The door opened and his two sons lumbered in. Tate was the taller of the two, although both were big, blond men like their father. Maddie resembled her mother, a delicate woman with big brown eyes and an easy smile. Gus had lost half his heart the day his wife had died. He wasn't about to surrender the other half without a fight.

"Did you find her?" Tate asked, closing the door behind him.

"Sit down, boys," Gus ordered.

They each grabbed a chair, Ben turning his around to straddle it. "What's Maddie done now?"

"She's gone after some felon in Texas. I traced her phone call to a hotel in Abilene."

"Texas?" Tate echoed. "Why the hell would she go all the way to Texas?"

"Because we couldn't interfere with her there," Ben replied. "You saw how angry she was after we commandeered her last takedown."

"Going all the way to Texas still seems a little extreme." Tate looked up at his father. "Who is she going after?"

"She didn't tell me. But since we don't have any out-of-state cases on our current docket, I'm assuming it's one of the unsolved cases."

Tate leaned back in his chair. "Well, that's a relief. If we couldn't find the guy, she won't either."

"She already did," Gus informed them, trying to keep his voice calm. "She called me this morning to tell me she's bringing him back to Chicago."

Ben frowned. "By herself?"

"That's right." Gus took a deep breath. "I already called the Abilene police, but they refused to intercede. Said she's probably already out of their jurisdiction. Same with the state police. The problem is that I don't know what route she's taking back here. She might be headed north on the highway through Oklahoma and Kansas, or east to Arkansas, or even taking backroads to avoid traffic and possible police check stops."

"That's what I'd do," Ben confirmed.

Though both the police and fugitive apprehension agents pursued felons, they operated in very different ways. Some cops disliked the methods bounty hunters used, or worse, thought of them as the competition. Staying a step ahead of the cops when bringing in a bail jumper made the job that much more complicated.

"Why in the hell did she go all the way to Texas?" Tate asked, his brow furrowed in confusion. "Who is she after?"

"Damned if I know," Gus replied. "But we're not going to sit around here wondering. I want you to go find her."

Tate threw his hands in the air. "Where? You just said she left Abilene."

"Dad," Ben interjected, before Gus could reply. "Maybe we should leave her alone. Let her find out once and for all if she's cut out for this business. Hell, she might even be good at it."

"Or she might end up dead," Gus bit out. "I'm not willing to take that chance, are you?"

Tate and Ben looked at each other. "No."

"Then find her. We've wasted enough time already." Gus closed his eyes and rubbed his hands over his face. He hadn't slept well since Maddie had turned up missing a week ago. And he knew he wouldn't sleep at all until he was certain she was safe.

In truth, nothing had been the same since their last argument. Gus's excuses for keeping her out of the business were beginning to sound hollow even to his ears.

Tate stood up. "Any suggestion where we might start looking for her?"

"The same place she found the fugitive—Abilene, Texas. Fly down there today and find out where she made the apprehension. Then trace her steps until you find her."

"That could take some time," Ben mused.

"Don't worry. I'll handle everything from this end. I've got tracers on both my home and business telephones, so if she calls again, we can pinpoint her location, perhaps even figure out her route."

"What if we do find her," Ben ventured, "and she refuses to come with us?"

Gus arched a brow. "You know what to do when faced with a reluctant apprehension, don't you?"

Ben's eyes widened. "You want me to handcuff my own sister and bring her home against her will?"

"I want you to do whatever is necessary to protect her. If that means throwing her over your shoulder while she's kicking and screaming, then so be it."

"Oh, boy," Tate muttered. "This should be one fun assignment."

"Just get it done," Gus ordered.

MADDIE GLANCED IN the rearview mirror of her Toyota Camry. Four hours out of Abilene, Tanner had fallen fast asleep. He still dozed in the back seat, his head drooped forward, bobbing at every bump and crevice in the pavement of the county line road.

She'd secured the handcuffs around the molded plastic hand-grip on the rear door opposite the driver's seat. Just far enough to prevent him from lunging at her.

Not that he seemed like the lunging type. Or the violent type. But she'd seen the calculating gleam in his eye when she'd returned his clothes to him. No doubt he was planning his escape. Or revenge.

But he was still in the car when she'd come out of the convenience store bearing breakfast. He'd even managed to change out of the rain slicker and into his jeans and torn shirt.

But he hadn't said a word to her since she'd paraded him through the hotel lobby, buck naked under the rain slicker.

Just as well, Maddie thought, reaching for the caffeinated soda she'd purchased at the last gas station. The less he said, the more peaceful the trip back to Chicago would be.

"Are we there yet?"

"Not even close," she replied, keeping her eyes on the long ribbon of road. "We crossed the state border into Oklahoma a while back. So only a thousand miles to go."

"I'm hungry."

"There's a sandwich and some chips in a bag on the seat next to you." She glanced at him in the rearview mirror. The thick, dark stubble shading his jaw definitely made him look dangerous. He caught her staring at him in the mirror and smiled. Her heart did a flip-flop as she hastily looked back at the road.

"You're too pretty to be a bounty hunter," he said after a long moment.

Just what she needed, another man telling her she wasn't cut out to make it in this business. Her hands flexed on the steering wheel. "Let's not talk about me."

"We've got over a thousand miles to kill," he reminded her. "We have to talk about something. How old are you?"

She hesitated a moment. "Twenty-five."

"Isn't that a little young to be out chasing criminals?"

"I caught you, didn't I?"

"But I'm not a criminal."

She rolled her eyes. "Aren't you getting a little tired of the 'I'm innocent' mantra?"

"How much money do you make?" he asked, ignoring her question.

"None of your business."

"It will be my business if the judge decides to garner your wages."

Her brows drew together as she glanced at him in the rearview mirror. "What are you talking about?"

"My civil lawsuit. I've decided to sue for punitive damages as well as loss of wages, emotional and physical suffering, alienation of affection...."

"Alienation of affection," she sputtered. "You've got to be kidding."

"Hey, you're the one who lured me up to your hotel room. And a man has certain expectations when a woman unbuttons his shirt, then pushes him onto the bed. I'll probably be scarred for life from that experience."

A blush warmed Maddie's cheeks. Thankfully, her back was to Blackburn so he couldn't see it. "You're just mad because I beat you at your own game."

"It wasn't a game to me, Maddie," he said quietly.

For a moment, she almost felt badly for hurting his feelings. Then she remembered who she was dealing with. The Kissing Bandit was a master of manipulation.

"You can sue me if you want, Blackburn," she said, as a bull snake slithered across the highway in front of her car. "But the judge will throw out the case as soon as he sees your record."

"The only thing I'm guilty of is lust in the first degree." He leaned his head back against the seat cushion and closed his eyes. "But last time I checked, that wasn't a crime."

Maddie didn't say another word for two hundred miles. Maybe her method of capture wasn't completely ethical. But she'd brought him down without harming him. She was certain he'd prefer her method to most of the other bounty hunters out there, including her brothers.

While Tanner munched on his sandwich, Maddie opened up the map across the steering wheel. She'd taken Highway 81 north through Oklahoma, then turned east on a county paved road after crossing into Kansas. But she hadn't counted on the proliferation of road construction that slowed her down every thirty miles. That's what she got for making an out-of-state fugitive apprehension in June. Despite the inconvenience, at least it was a learning experience.

Unfortunately, it was turning into one of those how-the-hell-did-I-get-into-this-mess learning experiences. An hour ago, she'd turned onto another county paved road. But the pavement had run out about twenty miles ago and now she was driving on gravel with no road signs on the horizon and no other cars in sight. There were plenty of cattle though. They stared at her as she breezed by their pastures. The sweet scent of freshly mown alfalfa hay seeped in through the air vents.

Maddie chewed her lower lip as her gaze moved from the map to the gravel road and back again. This little glitch in her schedule bothered her more than she wanted to admit. Why hadn't she called the highway department ahead of time to check on possible road construction? The gas gauge was now on the wrong side of the halfway mark and she had no idea where she was going. Or if she was even headed in the right direction.

"Lost already?" Tanner asked from the back seat.

"Of course not. I'm just reevaluating my itinerary."

He leaned forward to look out the window. "That grain silo looks familiar. Didn't we just drive by it a few minutes ago?"

"I know what I'm doing," she said, trying to sound confident. The problem was that she'd always had a lousy sense of direction. In Chicago, she navigated by landmarks, like the Sears Tower and Mc-

Donald's restaurants. Out here, she didn't recognize anything.

"Maybe we should stop and ask for directions," Tanner suggested.

As much as it galled her, Maddie knew she didn't have any other choice. It was either that or watch the cows go by until she ran out of gas.

"It looks like there's a farmstead about a half mile down the road."

She could see it, as well as the woman standing at the clothesline in the backyard. The woman turned as Maddie pulled into the winding dirt lane that led to a small farmhouse.

Leaving the basket of wet clothes on the lawn, the woman walked over to the driveway.

Maddie rolled down her window. "Hello."

"I'm not buying anything."

"We're not selling anything," Maddie explained.

"That includes religion," the woman interjected, folding her arms across her ample chest.

Tanner leaned forward. "Excuse me, ma'am. Do you have a telephone?"

"Yes," the woman replied, frowning as she leaned down toward the window for a closer look.

Maddie turned around to glare at him. "I'll do the talking."

Tanner ignored her. "Will you please call the police? I am the victim of a kidnapping." He tugged on the pink silk handcuffs, drawing her attention to the fact that he was chained to the car door.

The woman's eyes widened as she looked at Maddie. "Is that true?"

"Of course not," Maddie said lightly. "This is all part of a charity benefit. We kidnap eligible bachelors, then hold them hostage until someone forks over the ransom money. It's all for a good cause. We raised almost seven thousand dollars last year."

Tanner leaned forward. "Look, lady, she's making this all up. She tricked me into these handcuffs, then threatened me with pepper spray and a stun gun. Please call the local sheriff. My life may be in danger."

The woman looked from Tanner to Maddie, her brow furrowed.

"Here, I can prove it." Maddie reached into her black bag, retrieving a sheet of neon pink paper she'd printed up for just such an occasion. "This is a flyer that explains how the benefit works."

The woman skimmed the flyer, then laughed. "Oh, my, he's good, isn't he?"

"Wonderful," Maddie agreed. "He even chose not to shave this morning so he'd look the part."

"Incredible," Tanner breathed, his gaze fixed on Maddie.

She handed the flyer back to Maddie. "Well, isn't that clever? And certainly a more creative way to raise money than knocking on doors asking for handouts."

Maddie winked at the farm woman. "Part of the fun for the men is acting as if they've really been kidnapped. Believe me, he loved those kinky pink handcuffs when I first put them on him."

The woman's gaze turned speculative as she looked Tanner up and down. "So how much do you want for his ransom?"

"Well, I'm afraid he's already spoken for. I'm on my way to deliver him now, but I seem to have lost my way. Could you point me in the direction of the nearest town?"

"Sure." She pointed toward a stand of cedar trees. "Just head four miles past those trees, then take a right. Follow that road for another seventeen miles and you'll run straight into Crab Orchard."

"Thank you so much for your help," Maddie said. "We really appreciate it." Then she waved and drove off, her tires kicking up a plume of dust behind her. She glanced in the rearview mirror to see Tanner smiling at her.

"What's so funny?" she asked, suddenly uneasy.

"Nothing," he replied, sounding surprisingly cheerful for a man who just lost an opportunity to escape.

"She's not going to call the sheriff," Maddie informed him, just in case he was harboring any false hopes.

"Oh, I know that. Your creative powers continue to amaze me. In fact, everything about you amazes me."

"Thank you," she replied a little tentatively. Taking compliments from a felon usually wasn't part of the job description for a bounty hunter. But then, Tanner Blackburn didn't seem like your ordinary, run-of-the-mill criminal. He was well-spoken, intelligent and had an aura of integrity. Probably the very reason he'd so successfully evaded capture for so long.

She drove past the line of cedar trees, then glanced at the odometer so she wouldn't miss the four-mile mark. That's when she saw it. The glowing red Low Fuel light on the instrument panel.

"Crap," she breathed. The gas gauge needle was already flirting with the danger zone and she was smack in the middle of nowhere. Would she have enough fuel to drive twenty-two more miles?

At least now she knew why Tanner was smiling.

7

"I SURRENDER."

Maddie glanced at him through the rearview mirror. "What did you say?"

He gave her a slow smile. "I surrender, Maddie. I'm all yours."

"I know that," she said, her tone wary. "I'm just glad you finally realized it."

Tanner leaned back against the seat cushion, wondering why it had taken him so long to see the truth. The perfect woman was right in front of him. And he'd been spending way too much time trying to figure out how to get away from her. A natural reaction, considering his bruised masculine pride at being bested by a woman.

But what a woman.

Now that the shock of her amorous apprehension had started to fade, he realized that he really didn't want to escape, especially since he'd never find another woman like Maddie Griffin in Jamaica or anywhere else. Everything about her appealed to him. She was smart, independent and definitely sexy.

He closed his eyes, remembering that kiss they'd

shared in her hotel room. She'd been so incredibly hot, her mouth and her body igniting a fire inside of him that still burned. And she wasn't a clingy or needy woman, like so many of the women who had sought him through the *Texas Mail-Order Men* magazine. She was strong, self-sufficient.

A challenge.

Now he just had to figure out how to win her over. Prove to her that he was man enough to take all she had to give.

He shifted on the car seat, his legs cramped from sitting in one position so long. The digital clock on the front dash read 2:45 p.m. Cabe and Hannah would be at the barn by now, preparing for the three o'clock wedding ceremony. He wondered how long it had taken them to realize that Tanner would be a no-show. And how furious they would be when they discovered their wedding rings missing as well. If they'd just listened to him on the telephone this morning, he wouldn't be here with Maddie right now....

Maybe fate was on his side after all.

He watched Maddie nibble her lower lip as she navigated the car on the gravel roads. The speedometer crept up and up and up. She seemed to be under the mistaken assumption that the faster she drove, the less likely she'd be to run out of gas.

"I think we're going to make it," she said, as they crested a hill.

"Look out!" Tanner cried, as they met a tractor pulling a sixteen-row cultivator that spanned both edges of the gravel road.

Maddie slammed on the brake and the Toyota slid on the slippery gravel, narrowly missing the tractor as the car spun one-hundred and eighty degrees. It careened off the road and into the grassy ditch. A loud pop sounded when it finally came to a halt.

"Are you all right?" Maddie asked, twisting in her seat to look at him.

"Just a little bump on the head." He rubbed his temple with his free hand. "How about you?"

"I'm fine," she replied, her voice shaky and her hands still gripping the steering wheel.

They sat there in silence, the car tilted in the ditch at a sharp angle. The tractor had turned around in a field and was now slowly chugging toward them.

Maddie closed her eyes and leaned her head against the steering wheel. "Oh, hell."

Tanner smiled. No doubt about it. Fate was definitely on his side.

"IT'S FOR A CHARITY fund-raiser," Maddie explained, handing the mechanic a neon pink flyer. It was the same spiel she'd given the tow-truck driver who had hauled them and her crippled Toyota into town.

Crab Orchard was a tiny hamlet of just over five hundred people. The town catered to farmers and ranchers, with just enough businesses to provide the bare necessities, like food, beer and fertilizer—as well as a certified car mechanic.

Clayton Mobley was a full-time farmer who spent nights and weekends working on automobiles. He operated out of a massive steel-fabricated building separated from his house by a chain-link fence. His wife manned the telephones and did all the book-keeping. She was also the one who had towed Maddie's car into town.

"Wow," Clayton said, looking from the flyer to the handcuffs shackling Tanner's wrists. "I've never seen anything like this."

"So what's wrong with my car?" she asked, biting back her impatience. Surprisingly, Tanner hadn't gloated over her misfortune. In fact, he'd barely said a word since the accident. He stood beside her now, both wrists locked together in front of him, the empty pink ménage à trois cuff dangling between his legs.

His silence made her nervous.

Clayton tipped up his hat, revealing a streak of white forehead above his tan line. "You broke the front axle when you went into the ditch."

"Is that serious?"

He nodded. "You sure can't drive it until you get that axle replaced."

"When will that be?" she asked.

"Three, maybe four days."

Tanner smiled. "That long?"

She frowned up at him, apprehension skittering up her spine. His early indignation had disappeared. So had his protestations of innocence. He hadn't tried to plead his case to the tow-truck driver or to the mechanic. Instead, his sleek, powerful body loomed next to her, invoking images of a panther waiting to pounce on its prey.

"I don't keep parts for foreign cars in stock," Clayton explained. "Most people around here drive Fords or Chevys."

"Isn't there someplace else I can go that does keep Toyota parts in stock?" she asked, eager to find some way out of this predicament.

"Sure." He popped the tab on a soda can. "Wichita should have one."

"And how far is that from here?"

He sipped foam off the rim of the can. "Two hundred miles."

"To the west," Tanner added helpfully, the dimple in his chin winking at her.

Two hundred miles might as well be two thousand miles since she was headed in the opposite direction. Maddie closed her eyes, pinching the bridge of her nose between her fingers. She was already sleep-deprived, her brain fuzzy, and they weren't even close to Chicago yet.

Think, Maddie, think.

A bus or train was out of the question. There were too many people who could get in the way and possibly get hurt if Tanner tried to bolt. She could turn him over to the local sheriff, but that meant admitting that she couldn't do the job.

Unfortunately, it was starting to look that way.

The mechanic kept staring at the handcuffs, obviously fascinated with them. "So let me get this straight. You kidnap this guy, then get to keep him until someone pays his ransom?"

"That's right," Maddie said, aware she needed to keep up the playful facade if she didn't want to arouse suspicion. She reached out to pat her captive's broad shoulder. "He belongs to me."

Tanner turned to look at her, the hungry gleam in his eyes making her skin tingle. She knew without a doubt that he was thinking about last night. About the kiss they'd shared and the fantasies it had sparked.

Maddie had never shared such an intense physical attraction with another person before. She'd always scoffed at concepts like sexual chemistry and love at first sight. Not that she was stupid enough to fall in love with a felon. But she couldn't deny the sensual pull he had on her. So she just had to ignore it.

The mechanic's attention was still glued on the handcuffs. "Where would a guy find a pair of those?" He cleared his throat. "You know, just to have around as a conversation piece."

"I'll give them to you if you loan me a car to drive," Maddie said, not bothering to consider how she'd keep Blackburn under control without the cuffs.

Clayton shook his head, visibly disappointed. "Sorry, I don't have one to spare."

She sighed. "Then I guess we'll have to stay here until the part comes in."

"I'll put a rush order on it," the mechanic assured her, before taking a swig out of his soda can.

"No hurry," Tanner said, moving a step closer to Maddie. "But we'd appreciate it if you could point us in the direction of the nearest motel."

Maddie opened her mouth to protest, then realized she didn't have any other options. Although it did gall that Tanner seemed to think he was in charge. She'd have to put a stop to that nonsense.

The mechanic grinned. "Damn, some guys have all the luck. I wish a pretty woman would hold me hostage in a motel room."

"I'm completely at her mercy," Tanner replied.

She glanced up at him, certain she'd see a smirk stretched across that criminally handsome face. But he just stood there calmly awaiting her next order.

Right. If she believed that, she had no business pursuing a career in bail enforcement. This delay had upped the stakes considerably. Time was running out. The Kissing Bandit had been arraigned on the sixteenth of December. Today was June 10. Which meant Maddie had exactly six days left to bring him in if she wanted to collect the sizable fee for her father's agency.

She knew it, and she was certain Blackburn knew it, too. The delay would give him more time to plan an escape. Not that she'd ever let it happen. A Griffin always got his man—or, in this case, her man. She'd always prided herself on having more brains than her brothers, but willpower had never been an issue. Ben and Tate were slaves to their testosterone, while Maddie had maintained control of her head and her heart at all times.

And she wasn't about to stop now.

"Sorry to say we don't have any motels in Crab Orchard," Clayton said. "But you might be able to stay at Eleanor Cutter's house on Peach Street. She takes in folks sometimes."

"Like a bed-and-breakfast?" Maddie asked.

"I suppose you could call it that." He leaned forward. "Eleanor's a little strange. She has a reputation as the town loony. But most folks don't think she's dangerous or anything."

Wonderful. "And she rents out rooms?"

"Sure...sometimes." He set his soda can on a rusty upturned barrel. "Of course, none of her guests have ever come back to visit, but that doesn't really mean anything. Crab Orchard isn't exactly a resort spot."

"I guess we don't have any choice," Maddie muttered.

Clayton walked over to the open garage door.

"You'll find Eleanor's place three blocks west of the grocery store. Pink house with purple shutters. You can't miss it."

"Can you give me a call there when my car is ready?"

"Sure thing." The mechanic winked at them. "Have fun you two."

Tanner grinned. "We plan on it."

The undercurrent in his tone made Maddie's skin hot. She just wished she knew what he meant.

8

ELEANOR CUTTER'S HOUSE was a massive Victorian structure garishly painted in shades of pink, mauve and violet. It sprawled on the corner of the block, two towering oak trees standing sentinel on either side of the walk leading up to the house.

The slatted floor of the walk-around porch creaked as Tanner followed Maddie to the front door. She had her stun gun at the ready, obviously unaware that Tanner didn't plan to bolt. Just the opposite. He was looking forward to spending time alone with Maddie. Time to show her just how perfect they could be together.

She slipped the stun gun into her purse, then reached out and rang the doorbell, setting off an ominous gong. After the mechanic's cryptic description of the house owner, Tanner was somewhat surprised when a tiny woman with salt-and-pepper hair holding a matching salt-and-pepper toy poodle in her arms appeared at the door.

"Good afternoon, Ms. Cutter," Maddie began.

The poodle growled. Eleanor Cutter hushed the

dog, then narrowed her pale blue eyes. "Are you from the health department?"

"No," Maddie explained, one hand curled possessively around Tanner's arm. "We're just passing through and had some car trouble. Clayton Mobley told us you might have some rooms to rent."

She frowned. "Now why would that clunkhead say such a foolish thing?"

Maddie's face fell. "You mean you don't have any rooms?"

"I have *one* room. But it's not for just anybody."

One room. One bed? Tanner's heart beat double time at the possibilities.

"I'm willing to pay whatever you want," Maddie replied, sounding a little desperate. "This is something of an emergency. We'd only need the room for two, maybe three nights."

Eleanor frowned down at Tanner's hands. "What's this nonsense?"

"Oh, you mean the handcuffs," Maddie replied, digging into her bag.

Tanner assumed she was about to pull out another flyer. Maddie was not only sexy as hell, but damn creative. His body tightened when he thought of how much fun they could have with all that ingenuity, especially since he had a few creative ideas of his own.

"No," Eleanor countered. "I mean that man isn't wearing a wedding ring. And neither are you." Her nostrils flared. "This is a decent home, young woman. I don't rent out my room for weekend orgies. If you want to walk on the wild side, you'll have to go somewhere else. Crab Orchard is for proper, upstanding citizens."

The poodle barked his disapproval.

"You don't understand," Maddie replied. "My car broke down just outside of town and we're…"

"Married," Tanner finished for her.

Before Maddie could refute him, he lifted his cuffed wrists and brought his arms down around her, effectively trapping her between them. Then he pulled her close, her back pressed against his chest, her sweetly curved buttocks molded to his hips. His body instantly reacted to the contact, hardening almost to the point of discomfort. Her silky hair caressed his cheek and he inhaled the delectable scent that was uniquely Maddie.

She stiffened in his arms, but didn't try to escape. He could feel the tension in her body as she could no doubt feel his reaction to her nearness.

"You're married?" Eleanor said, skepticism snapping in her eyes. "Where are your wedding rings?"

"In my pocket," Tanner replied without a moment's hesitation. He had on the same denim jeans he'd worn to the wedding rehearsal, Cabe and Hannah's wedding bands still tucked safely in his pocket. "Our relationship has been on shaky ground almost from the moment we met. But we want to give our marriage one last shot."

Eleanor looked a little wistful. "You can't give up too soon."

Tanner nodded. "You're absolutely right. That's one of the reasons we decided to add a little spice to our love life by having Maddie kidnap me." He wiggled the chain dangling between his cuffed hands. "That's why I'm wearing these things. A little unorthodox for Crab Orchard, perhaps, but at this point I'm willing to try anything."

"You can say that again," Maddie hissed in a low voice.

He smiled, pleased that he'd caught her off guard. If he had his way, it wouldn't be the last time.

"Show her the rings, honey," he murmured in her ear, his lips nibbling the tender lobe.

He heard her suck in her breath. "I'm sure that's not necessary."

"Just reach into my pocket," he prodded, "so we can show Mrs. Cutter our wedding rings and give her peace of mind."

"It's *Miss* Cutter," Eleanor amended. "But you can call me Eleanor. And I would feel better if I saw the rings."

Maddie turned around in his arms until she was facing him. Her cheeks were flushed a bright pink as she wiggled her fingers into his front jeans pocket.

"There's nothing there," she said at last.

Tanner gazed down at her, molten desire pooling in his veins. "Are you sure about that?"

She snatched her hand out of his pocket, her cheeks flaming now. "Positive."

"Try the other pocket."

"This is ridiculous." Maddie dug her hand in his other pocket, then blinked. She pulled out two wide gold wedding bands.

"Put them on," Tanner murmured.

She looked up at him, then stepped back, but found herself still encircled in his arms. The cuffs on his hands prevented her from escaping.

"The rings, Maddie," he prodded.

She swallowed convulsively as she hastily slid the smaller ring onto the fourth finger of her left hand. For some irrational reason, he disliked the sight of it on her. It was a ring Cabe had chosen for Hannah. If anything, Maddie should be wearing a ring Tanner had bought for her. Someday, he vowed to himself, she'd be wearing his ring.

Tanner lifted his arms to release her, then stood still as she slid the larger gold band onto his ring finger. It was too tight, but she finally shoved it past his knuckle.

"There." Eleanor smiled. "That's much better. Now please follow me and I'll take you to the honeymoon suite."

Maddie frowned. "That's the only room you have available?"

"Yes." Eleanor scooped up her dog, then headed inside the house. "I usually only rent it out to newlyweds, but as you said before, this is something of an emergency."

"You have a lovely home," Maddie said politely, as Eleanor led them through the living room. The decor was modern and airy, with a few antiques sprinkled here and there to give it a homey touch.

"Thank you," Eleanor replied, walking to a rolltop desk near the staircase. "Mr. Tibbs and I like it."

"Mr. Tibbs?" Tanner echoed, wondering if Eleanor had a boarder. It made sense with such a huge house.

Eleanor patted the poodle's head. "This is Mr. Tibbs. But you can call him Harry."

"Hello, Harry," Tanner said.

The poodle barked at him.

"Good instincts, Harry," Maddie murmured under her breath.

"It's been so long since we've had any guests." Eleanor said, kissing the tip of the poodle's nose. "I'm afraid Harry is becoming a bit antisocial."

Maddie smiled. "Most dogs are protective of their owners."

Eleanor turned around to face her. "Harry isn't a dog. Not really."

Maddie and Tanner looked at each other. Then Tanner cleared his throat. "Then what is he?"

"The reincarnated spirit of my fiancé."

For a long moment, there was no sound in the house but the rhythmic ticking of the grandfather clock. Then Harry barked.

The sound made both Maddie and Tanner jump.

"There now," Eleanor said, scratching behind Harry's ears. "I've told you there's no reason to keep it a secret. These nice people understand about true love."

Tanner no longer wondered why Clayton had referred to Eleanor Cutter as the town loony. Despite the woman's apparent contentment, he felt a little sorry for her, and more than a little unnerved by the sentience shining in Harry's milky brown eyes.

"Now, how long did you say you needed a room?" Eleanor asked.

Maddie unconsciously moved a step closer to Tanner. "Two, possibly three nights."

"If you stay for a week, you can get the discount. Ten percent off the regular room rate."

"What is the regular room rate?" Maddie asked.

"Three hundred dollars."

Her jaw dropped. "A night?"

"It's a little steep, I know," Eleanor conceded. "But Harry insisted that we keep up with inflation. He's always been a whiz with numbers."

Tanner looked at Maddie and saw her lips twitch. He clenched his jaw to keep from laughing. Only the harder he tried to contain it, the greater the urge to laugh became.

Maddie glanced up at him, amusement dancing in her beautiful eyes. And in that moment, he knew he was actually falling in love with her.

Eleanor frowned up at them. "Is it warm in here? You both look a little flushed."

"Not at all," Maddie said, a very unladylike snort escaping her.

Tanner moved closer to her. "I think my wife and I are just a little giddy at the thought of spending time alone together."

Maddie nodded, obviously not trusting herself to speak.

"Well, then Harry and I'd better show you up to your room."

BY THE TIME THEY'D CLIMBED two flights of stairs, Maddie had gained control of her temporary attack of hysteria. It was Tanner's fault. He'd completely caught her off guard when he'd captured her in his arms. She tried to tell herself that the attraction pulsating between them was perfectly normal. Especially since it had been eons since she'd been held like that by a man.

All she had to do was ignore this odd affinity she had for the man. Pretend it didn't exist. As soon as she got to Chicago, she could forget about Tanner Blackburn and the disconcerting effect he had on her.

Eleanor ushered them into a large room with dormer windows. Stepping over the threshold was like stepping into the past. An antique bed with a cast-iron headboard dominated the room. A lacy, white coverlet and an abundance of hand-embroidered throw pillows issued an irresistible invitation to sink into all of that plush softness.

A large stone fireplace encased the north wall, bracketed by long windows. Stained-glass insets bordered the top of every window in the room, casting soft rays of amber, pink and blue over the polished oak floor. Maddie couldn't imagine a more beautiful room.

Or a more romantic one.

"Well?" Eleanor asked, a knowing smile on her lined face. "What do you think?"

"It's lovely," Maddie said, slowly turning around to admire the moldings on the ceiling and walls.

"There are plenty of towels in the bathroom," Eleanor said, nodding toward the adjoining room. "The room should be fully stocked, but please let me know if you need anything."

Tanner walked over to the bed. "I think we have everything we need."

"Then I'll say good night." Eleanor's blue eyes twinkled. "And good luck."

Luck. Maddie could definitely use a little of that right about now. She walked over to the door and turned the ancient lock. Then she turned to face her captive.

Tanner sat down on the bed, then fell back into the downy coverlet, sinking halfway into the mattress. "This is great. You should try it."

"I think I'll stay right here, thank you."

She watched as he pushed his elbows into the mattress, turning to one side, then the other before flopping onto his back again.

"Maddie?"

"Yes?"

"I can't get up."

She swallowed an irritated sigh, then walked over to the bed. "You're making this much harder than necessary."

"That's funny. I was just thinking the same thing about you."

She reached down and grabbed his broad shoulders to pull him upright. Instead, his foot snaked around her ankles and threw her off balance. She fell forward, landing right on top of him. They both toppled back onto the mattress.

In an instant, Tanner rolled so that she lay underneath him, pinned by his large body. His hands were still cuffed, now caught between them. She could feel the broad tips of his fingers pressed against the top of her thighs.

"Get off of me," she ordered, furious with herself for letting him catch her off guard again.

"Not yet," he said, shifting so his body fit naturally against her own. "I'm enjoying the moment."

"I think you're forgetting I've still got a stun gun in my purse."

"And I think you're forgetting how much we both enjoyed our last kiss. Maybe I should remind you."

She opened her mouth to protest, but he covered her lips with his own before she could make a sound. He could have reveled in her temporary helplessness, taking his revenge by ravaging her mouth. Instead, he gave her a tender, sweet kiss that made her traitorous body soften underneath him. His fingers lightly brushed her thighs, igniting tiny sparks of desire deep inside of her.

A moan escaped her throat. She couldn't let him have control. But his powerful body proved too strong to dislodge, and his determination too strong for her to ignore what he was doing to her. His mouth molded against her own, sipping her lips, gently urging her to return his passion.

She closed her eyes, telling herself not to panic, or to let Tanner know how he was affecting her. The kiss couldn't last forever. She'd just lay here like a corpse until he finally got tired of trying to resuscitate her.

Maddie kept her body as still as stone, then felt Tanner smile against her mouth. He'd obviously figured out her strategy. But instead of stopping, he deepened the kiss. Tracing his tongue across the seam of her mouth and emitting a low, hungry growl deep in his throat.

Despite Maddie's determination, her body betrayed her. Her nipples hardened and a sweet pressure burned between her legs. Another tiny moan emanated from her as his fingers traced tiny circles on her thighs, coming perilously close to intimate contact. The lack of oxygen was making her dizzy. That was the only explanation for her reaction to his touch. His tongue continued to trace the seam of her mouth insistently, begging entrance.

She gave it to him. Then her spine arched upward, seemingly of its own accord, seeking relief in the pressure of his hard body against her own. Rational thought fled as Tanner seduced her with his tongue. The only thing that mattered was this moment.

"Let me touch you," he said, his voice husky.

Yes, her mind whispered, as her fingers reached up and fumbled for the key she'd strung on a chain around her neck. She couldn't resist him. Better to admit the truth than delude herself any longer. No doubt he had this effect on all his women.

All his victims. A cold wave of disgust washed over her. The Kissing Bandit thought he could seduce her into submission. Time to prove him wrong.

Tanner rose above her as she pulled the key over her head, giving her just enough room to bring her knee up sharply between his legs.

He gasped, then fell like a rock onto his side. Maddie sat up as he made gagging noises in the back of his throat.

"Sorry." She rose to her feet hastily, finger combing her mussed hair. "I didn't want you to kiss me."

"Don't worry," he gurgled, taking a deep gasp of air. "It won't happen again."

"Good." She walked over to the window, her cheeks burning. Some bounty hunter. She'd not only let Tanner trick her into submission, she'd let him kiss her. Even worse, she'd kissed him back.

Why had Maddie assumed she'd be immune to him? They called him the Kissing Bandit for a reason. From now on she needed to keep her guard up and keep her distance. If he couldn't reach her, he couldn't kiss her. A few days from now, they'd be back on the road. As soon as she hit Chicago, she'd turn him over to the authorities. It was that simple. It had to be.

She turned around to face him. Tanner was sitting up on the edge of the bed now, his handsome face still etched with pain. A barb of guilt pricked her. "Are you injured?"

"No." He took a deep breath. "But you've traumatized me for life. I'll never be able to kiss a woman again."

"Since that seems to be the source of all your problems, it might be a blessing in disguise."

"Funny," he said, wincing as he shifted on the mattress, "it doesn't feel like a blessing."

She folded her arms over her chest. "Perhaps now you'll realize that I'm a dangerous woman, Mr.

Blackburn. If you want to avoid further injury, I suggest you do everything I tell you until we reach Chicago.''

"Dangerous," he murmured, letting the word linger in the air between them. "Yes, Maddie, you're definitely dangerous. I knew that from the moment you handcuffed me. But you're also something else."

"What?" she asked, not liking the half smile now curving his mouth.

"Tempted."

9

THE NEXT DAY, TANNER LAY cuffed to the bed in the honeymoon suite, wondering where he'd gone wrong. The women in his past had melted like butter whenever he'd turned on the charm. Only Maddie didn't melt, she sizzled. And he'd gotten burned.

She might have had a knee-jerk reaction to his kiss last night, but her body had told him what she refused to admit. She wanted him as much as he wanted her. Tanner had spent most of the day reliving the moments before her knee had effectively ended his fantasies.

That second kiss had rocked him to his soul. When her lips had finally opened for him, he'd found heaven inside. So sleek and sexy that his mouth tingled at the memory. And the way her body had moved against him left no doubt that he'd finally breached that brick wall she'd erected against him.

But the tender ache in his groin reminded him that taking the offensive wasn't the best strategy. He needed to conduct a more subtle campaign—nice and slow so she'd let her guard down around him.

Then, when he had her exactly where he wanted, he'd coax her into a state of surrender.

He stared up at the ceiling fan, his wrists still shackled to the headboard. Maddie had gone downstairs to make arrangements for dinner. At least that had been her excuse. She'd found reasons to be in and out of the honeymoon suite all day.

He smiled, remembering the telling flush in her cheeks when he'd accused her of being tempted by him. She'd hotly denied it, then fled the room. Beneath that tough, sexy swagger, Maddie Griffin was all woman. Now he just needed to figure out the right way to make her forget she was a bounty hunter.

A direct pursuit obviously wasn't the route to take. Not if he wanted to protect his ability to have children someday. Better to make her come to him. Woo her into a sense of security.

Tanner inhaled the clean, sweet air blowing in from the open window. He hadn't felt this alive in years. He should have taken a vacation a long time ago. Granted, Crab Orchard wasn't Jamaica, and finding himself handcuffed to a bed wasn't the same as sipping banana daiquiris on a white sand beach.

But there was no place he'd rather be.

He heard a key turning in the lock, and his pulse kicked up a notch in anticipation.

Let the games begin.

MADDIE SLIPPED THE KEY back into her pocket then reached for the doorknob. The wedding band on her finger gleamed, reflecting the overhead hallway light. Pretending they were husband and wife had thrown her off balance. She had been jittery all day, finding one excuse after another to avoid Tanner.

Her reaction to him was utterly ridiculous. The man wasn't a magician. He certainly couldn't seduce her against her will. Still, he had kissed her twice. And that last kiss had almost evolved into something more. Something that still made Maddie's heart pound in her chest when she thought about it.

"So stop thinking about it," she told herself fiercely, propping the supper tray on one hip. She couldn't go in there until she'd sorted it all out in her mind. Tanner Blackburn was a felon. The notorious Kissing Bandit. He belonged behind bars.

Only her firm convictions about the man had begun to fray around the edges. There were just too many unanswered questions.

Like why did he have two wedding rings in his pocket? Rings were traditionally carried by the best man before a wedding. Was it remotely possible that he'd been telling her the truth?

And why had he gone out of his way to make things easier for her? Like asking the mechanic the directions to the nearest motel and telling Eleanor they were married.

Nothing he did made any sense. Not for a guilty

man. And she couldn't let herself consider the alternative.

Realizing their supper would grow cold before she resolved her doubts, Maddie took a deep breath, then opened the door to the honeymoon suite and walked inside.

Tanner lay stretched out on the bed, all six feet two inches of delectable male. "Hey, gorgeous."

"I hope you're hungry," she said, setting the tray on the small table by the window. "Eleanor is an aspiring gourmet."

"She probably wants to make sure we keep up our strength."

Maddie ignored his innuendo, pulling the table up next to bed. "The champagne was her idea, not mine."

She worked the plastic stopper with her fingers, aware of Tanner's gaze on her. Despite her vow to maintain a professional demeanor around him, a hot flush spread over her body. The cork popped, hitting the wall above Tanner's head, and champagne bubbled out the top of the bottle.

She held it over a champagne flute, catching the overflow before it spilled. Then she filled the other flute and handed it to him.

"Thank you," he said, swinging his legs over to sit on the side of the bed. He picked up a fork, the chain linking his wrists together clinking against the fine china.

"Here," she said, removing the necklace with the key from around her neck. She inserted the key into the lock mechanism of the cuff on his right wrist. Her fingers brushed over his hand as the cuff opened, and he caught them and held them firmly in his grasp.

"Thank you again." Heat radiated from both his fingers and his eyes.

Maddie had to force herself not to pull her hand away. She didn't want him to think he intimidated her, or threatened her. Fortunately, he didn't know how hard her heart pounded in her chest or about the fluttery sensation in the pit of her stomach.

"You're welcome," she said, casually withdrawing her hand.

His left wrist was still chained to the headboard, but he had enough leeway to stand up and pull a chair to the table for her. Then he held it out for her until she took a seat, acutely aware of the way his hand brushed over her shoulder.

Tanner sat back down on the bed, watching her as she buttered a French roll.

"Aren't you hungry?" she asked, realizing he hadn't touched his food.

He gazed into her eyes. "Starving."

She dropped her gaze to her plate. "Then you'd better eat because this is all you're going to get tonight."

He hesitated a moment, then finally turned his attention to the plate in front of him.

Maddie breathed a silent sigh of relief.

Tanner took a bite of the salmon fillet, then closed his eyes in appreciation. "This is delicious. I wonder if Eleanor would give me the recipe."

She laughed. "You cook?"

"Don't look so surprised," he chided with a devastating smile. "I took a few classes after my sister moved in with me. She survived my experiments in the kitchen and I expanded her diet to include more than jelly beans and diet soda."

Maddie broke another roll apart, then slathered it with fresh butter. "I'm a disaster in the kitchen. My father seems to think cooking talent is handed down genetically, like eye color and freckles. My mother was a great cook, so he thought I was just rebelling."

"Lauren regularly sets off the smoke alarm," Tanner replied, after taking another bite of fish. "Her specialty is blackened grilled cheese sandwiches."

"Mine, too." She took a sip of champagne. The bubbles tickled the back of her throat as she relaxed against the back of the chair.

"I'm going to miss cooking for her." Tanner looked hastily down at his plate, as if embarrassed by the disclosure.

Maddie took another sip of champagne, watching him over the rim of the flute. The dark whiskers shadowing his jaw gave him the dangerous look of an outlaw that she found strangely exciting. The biceps in his right arm flexed as he swiped the roll over the sauce on his plate. Her mouth watered as he devoured the roll in two bites, then licked the buttery crumbs from his fingertips.

Those same fingers had caressed her thighs last night while they'd kissed, the rough strokes sending tingles throughout her body. Part of the illicit thrill had been knowing his hands were locked together, that he couldn't really do anything she didn't want him to do. But Tanner had used more than his fingers to arouse her. He'd used his supple mouth and his powerful body.

Her gaze fell to his broad shoulders, then his chest as a delicious warmth spread over her skin. She wanted to feel that thrill again. Let him touch her one more time.

What if he was telling the truth? What if she was locked in a room with a gorgeous man...who was completely innocent? Then Tanner looked up at her, and his magnetic blue eyes were anything but innocent.

She pushed her plate away, then dabbed at her mouth with the napkin. No matter what fantasies she found herself weaving around this man, he was the Kissing Bandit.

He just had to be.

TANNER TOOK A SIP OF champagne, his gaze never leaving Maddie. Her lips looked so soft and inviting.

The woman might not know how to cook but she tasted wonderful. He opened his mouth to tell her just that, then closed it again. Nice and slow, he reminded himself.

"Lauren is starting college at Duke this fall," he said, attacking his green beans almondine. "So I'll have to get used to baching it again."

"Good school. You must have had to bilk a lot of ladies out of their bank accounts to cover the tuition."

"Actually, she's on a full scholarship. You can check with the university if you don't believe me."

"I just might."

He stopped chewing, then swallowed, trying not to choke. This was the first time she'd ever admitted the possibility that he *might* be telling the truth. Even if she didn't mean it, Tanner knew it was a step in the right direction.

"So what's on the agenda after dinner?" he asked, setting down his fork.

She leaned back in her chair. "You could entertain me with stories of your adventures as the Kissing Bandit."

"I'd rather hear how you became a bounty hunter."

She gave him a reluctant smile. "Unlike cooking, the bounty hunter biz *is* in my blood. I'm just following in the footsteps of my father and brothers."

Tanner nodded. "So who is the most notorious criminal you've caught?"

"You. Actually, you're the first criminal I've caught."

He smiled. "So you're a bounty hunter virgin?"

A flush suffused her cheeks. "Not anymore."

"I'm honored that you let me be your first."

She narrowed her eyes. "You're doing it on purpose."

"What?"

"Trying to fluster me. It won't work."

"Good." He laid his napkin on the table. "Because I have a proposition for you."

She scowled. "I thought I made my feelings about any *propositions* quite clear last night."

"Definitely," he said, squirming slightly at the memory. "But this is a different kind of proposition. Are you a betting woman?"

She hesitated. "Occasionally."

"Since we have the night to kill, no television or other...distractions, how about a game of poker?"

She leaned forward, unwittingly giving him a view of her creamy cleavage. "What are the stakes?"

He cleared his throat, then forced his gaze back up to her face. "A telephone call. I'm entitled to at least one, aren't I?"

"I'm sure the authorities at the Cook County jail will allow you to use a telephone."

Tanner smiled at her. "Chicken?"

She tipped up her chin. "Of course not. But we don't even have a deck of cards."

He reached over and pulled open the top drawer of the nightstand. "I did some snooping while you were downstairs. Eleanor wasn't joking when she said the room was fully stocked. Guess what I found?"

"A deck of cards?"

"That's right. As well as a box of condoms." He watched her take a sip of champagne, her tongue darting out to lick a stray drop off her lower lip. "We could play with those if you prefer."

She set down the glass then cleared the plates off the table. "Give it up, Blackburn, and just deal the cards."

"So you agree to my terms?" he challenged. "If I win, I get to make one phone call?"

"I suppose that's fair," she said, as he shuffled the cards. "But what if I win?"

"I'll do anything you want, Maddie," he replied, his voice low and suggestive. "Just tell me your heart's desire."

He bit back a smile at the blush that crept up her neck. Obviously, he wasn't the only one who had been reliving that kiss last night. If he could just get her to trust him, to believe him. Not only because it would mean his freedom, but because he wanted Maddie to see him for himself, not as some phantom felon called the Kissing Bandit.

"What shall we use for chips?" he asked.

"I have an idea." She walked into the adjoining bathroom, then emerged a moment later with a basket full of colored bath beads. "The yellow ones will be worth a dollar. The blue ones worth five. And the red ones worth ten."

Tanner placed the deck on the table while Maddie divvied out the bath beads. "Do you want to cut to see who deals?"

"Of course." She cut the cards, revealing a queen.

Tanner pulled up a jack.

"I win," she said with a smile, seating herself across from him. "Get used to it."

He watched her expertly shuffle the cards. "What are we playing?"

"Five card draw," she announced, neatly dealing out five cards for each of them. "Deuces wild."

He picked up his cards, fanning them out to reveal two kings, an ace, a six and an eight.

"It's your bet, Tanner."

He realized then that she called him by his last name when she was feeling flustered or threatened, and by his first name when she felt more in control and secure. In poker they called it a tell. *Interesting.* And possibly something he could use to his advantage.

"One dollar." He placed a yellow bath bead in the center of the table.

"I'll meet that and raise you five," she replied, adding a yellow and blue bath bead to the pot.

He tossed another blue bead to the center of the table. "Three cards, please." He kept the two kings in his hand, discarding the rest.

Maddie dealt out three cards to him. "Dealer takes one."

Tanner slowly fanned out his cards, his heart beating erratically in his chest. It might be due to the fact that he'd just picked up a third king in his hand. But it was more likely Maddie was to blame. He watched her over his cards, mesmerized by the concentration he saw on her face. Her perfect white teeth nipped at her lush lower lip, making him wish he could do the same.

He imagined himself unbuttoning the prim pink blouse she wore to reveal the creamy soft skin underneath. Those tight denim jeans of hers had fanned his fantasies all day. He wanted to peel them off, eager to see her sleek bare legs again. For one brief instant, he envisioned them wrapped around his waist.

"Tanner?"

He blinked. "What?"

"It's your bet."

Now it was his turn to blush as he tossed two blue bath beads on the center of the table. "It'll cost you ten more to stay in this hand."

She studied her cards for a moment, then reached

for two red bath beads. "I'll see your ten and raise you fifteen."

"Hey, wait a minute. Don't we have any betting limits?"

"No limits," she countered, her voice turning husky. Almost seductive. "That's how I like to play."

He stared at her, unable to believe she was actually flirting with him. Or was this another game? "I think you're bluffing."

She smiled. "It will cost you fifteen to prove it."

He smiled back at her, realizing she liked the thrill of competition as much as he did. Maybe this was a game they could both win. He added three blue bath beads to the pot, then dropped in another red bath bead. "First I'm going to raise you ten more."

"Now who's bluffing?" She dropped a red and blue bath bead onto the table. "It will cost you five more to stay in the game." She arched one dark brow. "Are you man enough?"

His gaze held hers across the table while his body answered her challenge of its own accord. He wondered how she'd react if he showed her exactly how manly he was feeling at the moment. Instead, he tossed a blue bead into the pot. "Okay. It's time to lay down and show me what you've got, Maddie."

She fanned her cards faceup in front of her. "Full house. Jacks over eights."

He folded his cards. "It's all yours."

She laughed as she scooped up the pot. "You won't even last an hour at this rate."

"The game's not over yet." He picked up the deck and started shuffling. "Besides, I've got incredible stamina."

She looked up at him, her eyes wary. "You're doing it again."

"Doing what?"

"You know…the double entendres."

"I'm just making conversation," he said innocently. "I can't help the way your mind works."

She flipped her hair over her shoulder. "Just deal the cards, Blackburn."

He bit back a smile. Nice and slow. That was definitely the right strategy. And he was determined to come out the winner. "Okay, seven card stud, nothing wild."

Maddie neatly arranged her bath beads by color. "My favorite."

Forty-five minutes later, Tanner had eight dollars worth of bath beads left. Maddie had won enough to indulge in a lifetime of bubble baths.

"Four of a kind," she announced, laying her cards on the table.

Tanner muttered an oath as he tossed his cards down. "Where did you learn to play poker?"

"Miss Emily's Finishing School for Young Ladies," she replied, scooping up the pot. "Most of the girls were from affluent East Coast families. I was a bounty hunter's daughter from Chicago. Poker was a great equalizer. I earned enough money to buy the right clothes so I wouldn't look like such an outsider."

"Finishing school?" Tanner smiled. "Somehow I just can't see you balancing books on your head and learning to pour tea."

"It was my father's idea," she said with a grimace. "He'd found Miss Emily's delinquent brother, who had jumped bail in Illinois. She had mortgaged her school to secure the bond and would have lost everything. Miss Emily showed her gratitude by giving me free room and board at the school."

"Lucky you."

"Yeah," she muttered, reaching for the cards. "Lucky me."

His hand covered hers, preventing her from picking up the deck. "Look, it's pretty obvious I only have enough bath beads left for one more hand. Let's make it a big one. All or nothing."

She pulled her hand out from under his. "Or you could just concede."

"Chicken?"

"You're repeating yourself, Tanner. I think you're trying to bait me."

"I'm just trying to make it interesting. Look, Maddie, I will concede you're the better poker player. But this is important to me." He looked into her eyes.

She hesitated for a moment. "Okay. But you're going to lose."

"I'll take my chances."

She pushed the deck toward him. "Since it's the last hand, I'll let you call it."

"Indian chief," he announced.

She laughed. "That's not a real game!"

"That's what I'm calling." He dealt one card facedown to each of them. "Now remember, you can't look at your card. You have to hold it, face out, on your forehead." He demonstrated with his own card. "Like this."

"You look ridiculous." She pushed her card away. "I'm not playing."

"Does this mean you forfeit?"

"No serious poker player would ever play this game."

"I can call whatever I want. No limits, remember?"

She sighed, then picked up her card, holding it front of her forehead so Tanner could see it.

"I hate to say it, Maddie. But this is one hand you're going to lose."

"I feel like an idiot."

He let his gaze take a leisurely trip over the length of her body. "You look gorgeous."

She shifted in chair. "Quit bluffing, Blackburn, and play the game."

"It's your bet. I've already told you what I want if I win. One phone call. What do you want, Maddie?"

She licked her lips. "Your total cooperation until we get to Chicago."

He definitely intended to cooperate. "Deal."

Her brown eyes narrowed. "Do you really mean it? Because if there's one thing I can't stand, it's a welcher."

"You have my word," he replied, "whatever that means to you."

"Not much," she muttered. "Maybe I should ask for something more tangible." She wiggled her left ring finger. "Like this nice gold wedding band."

"You're just stalling because I have a fantastic card."

Maddie looked up at his forehead. "Don't get your hopes up."

"We've each made our bet. Now let's lay down our card on the count of three, okay."

"Okay. One…"

"Two," Tanner intoned.

"Three," they said at the same time, each slapping their card on the table.

"A deuce," Maddie exclaimed, looking down at her card. "A lousy deuce of spades!"

"Looks like I win," Tanner said, pointing to his card. It was the four of hearts.

She frowned. "So that's why it was so easy for you to wager your cooperation. You knew I'd lose."

"Hey, that's what poker is all about." He leaned back in his chair. "I hope you have enough change for my phone call. It's long distance."

"I'll put it on my credit card," she replied. "On one condition."

"What?"

"I'll tell you as soon as we find a telephone."

10

MADDIE STOOD IN THE FRONT parlor, the stun gun in one hand and a telephone receiver in the other. It was after ten o'clock and Eleanor had gone to bed. Harry the poodle was still awake and sat on a rug in front of the television set watching CNN.

She could see Tanner through the open French doors of the study, where she'd secured the handcuffs to the leg of a heavy wooden desk that dominated the room. He sat on the floor, holding the extension phone with his free hand. They both listened silently to the ringing on the other end of the line.

"C'mon, Lauren," he breathed into the phone. "Pick up."

Was this Lauren really his sister? Or a girlfriend? Maybe even a partner in crime. Maddie had insisted on listening in on his conversation. Not only to make certain he wasn't calling for someone to rescue him, but to discover if he'd really been telling the truth about having a sister.

The phone picked up after the fifth ring. "Hello?"

The woman on the other end of the line sounded young and breathless.

"Hey, Lauren," Tanner said. "Sounds like I caught you in the middle of your aerobics routine."

She laughed, though it sounded a little strained. "I am a little out of breath. How are you, Tanner? How's Jamaica? Found any babes, yet?"

Maddie's grip tightened on the receiver. *Jamaica.* Tanner had told her he'd been planning a vacation. Claimed that she'd ruined it by nabbing him. Of course, she believed that's where he was taking his poor, deceived bride for the honeymoon. But why would his sister ask if he'd found any babes if she knew he was on his honeymoon?

Then another question occurred to her. One that sent a cold shiver down her spine. If Tanner had been the groom, wouldn't his sister have been at the wedding? Wouldn't she question why he'd left the bride standing at the altar?

Unless this sister was completely in the dark about his illegal Lothario activities.

Maddie rubbed her temple. All the possibilities were giving her a headache. She didn't even want to think about the worst-case scenario. That Tanner had been telling her the truth. That she'd nabbed the wrong man.

"I'm fine," he replied. "But I decided to skip Jamaica and opt for Kansas instead."

She tensed, ready to end the call if he divulged any more information.

"Kansas?" Lauren said. "Are you nuts? Is there

anything in Kansas that can possibly compare to a beautiful tropical paradise?''

Maddie looked up to see Tanner staring at her. The heat in his eyes burned through to her soul.

"Oh, you'd be surprised," he said softly into the phone.

"Well, when are you coming home?"

He shrugged. "It will probably be a few days."

Try five to ten years. Maddie wondered how Lauren would handle the news of her brother's capture. She sounded like a nice girl. But then, as Maddie knew from recent personal experience, appearances could be deceiving.

"So what's new?" Tanner asked, leaning back against the desk.

"Oh, not much," Lauren replied. "Dad called. He just broke up with girlfriend number fifty-four. Oh, that reminds me. Ronnie's back in town."

Tanner frowned. "When did this happen?"

"He stopped by the house after I got back from my camping trip. It seems the missionary life doesn't suit our brother after all."

"So what's he planning to do now?"

"He seems pretty excited about the farmland Grandma left us in Iowa. He told me he's planning to take a road trip up to Hominy and see what it's worth."

"Did you tell him I'm having it appraised? We

should be getting the report from the real estate company soon."

"You know Ronnie," Lauren said with a sigh. "He can't stay in one place for too long. He's probably in Iowa right now."

"Yeah, I know Ronnie."

"Sometimes it's hard to believe you two are twins."

Maddie blinked. *Twins?*

"Hey, Tanner, hold on a minute," Lauren said, as a low male voice sounded in the background.

Maddie saw Tanner tense. He sat up. "Is someone there with you?"

"Just a friend," Lauren replied. Unlike her brother, she didn't make a good liar.

"A male friend?" he persisted. "In the house with you? Alone?"

A sigh sounded over the line. "Tanner, I'm eighteen years old."

His shoulders tensed. "And I'm a man. I know how men think. I want him out of there. Now."

"It's nothing serious," his sister assured him. "Jon and I met on the camping trip. We just started dating a few days ago."

"Dating?" He squeezed the receiver so tight that veins bulged in his hand. "Why would you want to start dating when you're leaving for college in a few weeks?"

"It's just a summer fling," she said softly into the

phone, obviously not wanting to let Jon in on that little secret.

"A fling," Tanner rasped, raking a hand through his hair. "My little sister is having a *fling*. I don't like it, Lauren. I don't like it one bit."

"I think you're just bummed out on romance because Hannah dumped you for Cabe."

Maddie stared at Tanner, now thoroughly confused. *Hannah?* Who was Hannah? And since when did a woman dump the Kissing Bandit?

"I'm not bummed out," he replied, sounding a little calmer. "And Hannah didn't dump me. We came to a mutual understanding."

"Sorry." Lauren sounded contrite. "Oh, I almost forgot. Hannah called and left a message on the answering machine Saturday. She didn't sound too happy."

"I don't want to talk about Hannah. I want to talk about this guy you're seeing."

"I should probably go. Jon is waiting."

"Jon can keep waiting. In fact, he can..."

"Have a great time in Kansas," his sister interjected loudly, drowning out his words. "Bye."

Tanner leaned forward. "Lauren, wait...."

Maddie heard the click in her ear, then saw Tanner frown down at the receiver.

She hung up her end, then walked into the study. "So that's Lauren?"

He heaved a frustrated sigh as he dropped the receiver back into the cradle. "That's Lauren."

Maddie leaned against the doorway, studying him closely. "Your big brother act didn't go over too well."

"Tell me about it." He rubbed one hand over the thick shadow of whiskers on his jaw. "Lauren's always had a mind of her own."

"Anything wrong with that?"

He looked up at her, then grinned, his dimple flashing in his chin. "Nothing. I like a woman who knows what she wants and goes after it. I like it a lot."

She shifted on her feet, aware that the conversation had somehow switched from his sister to her. "Most men feel differently."

"I'm not like most men," he replied.

She knew that already. No other man had ever had this effect on her. Every nerve in her body tingled when he looked at her like that.

Maddie knew her feelings for him were shifting. It was alarming, intriguing—although she wasn't quite ready to admit she'd made a mistake, even if he had been telling the truth about having a sister. Criminals had families, didn't they?

She'd always thought of the Kissing Bandit as heartless though. Always thought that any man who could deceive women, using their affections against them, couldn't have tender feelings for any woman, even his own sister. But Tanner's distress at Lauren's social life was very real.

"Let's go back to the room," she said, still trying to fit this new piece into the puzzle that was Tanner Blackburn. "It's late. And I have a feeling Lauren can take care of herself."

"My sister thinks I'm overprotective," Tanner said, as he watched Maddie unlock the cuff around the desk leg. "I suppose you agree with her."

She smiled. "Hey, I've got two older brothers myself. It can be a little suffocating for a girl."

He rose awkwardly to his feet, his ripped shirtsleeve giving her a glimpse of the finely honed muscles in his arm. "There are a lot of jerks out there. I just don't want her to get hurt."

She thought about her family. "Sometimes lack of trust can hurt even more."

He turned to look at her. "Are you speaking from experience?"

Maddie mentally kicked herself for revealing too much. Tanner seemed to have an uncanny knack for making her do that. "Forget I said anything."

He slowly shook his head. "I can't forget anything you say, Maddie. I know it sounds crazy, but you're in my thoughts both day and night." Then his gaze dropped to her mouth. "Especially at night."

Her heart skipped a beat. "Is this the Kissing Bandit talking?"

His gaze rose to meet hers. "What do you think?"

"I think we should go to bed."

Heat flashed in his blue eyes.

"Alone," she blurted, her cheeks on fire. "It's late. I'm tired. You're tired." She glanced at the poodle. "I'm sure Harry's tired, too."

At the sound of his name, Harry turned his head and barked.

A slow smile eased across Tanner's handsome face. "I guess I can't argue with both of you."

"Smart man," she replied, steering him toward the staircase. The phone call bothered her more than she wanted to admit. Not because of what Tanner said, but more because of what he didn't say. He didn't mention his apprehension at all, or the fact that he was on his way to a Chicago jail. He didn't ask Lauren to defend him or to back up his story or even call a lawyer.

The only question was: why?

"Who's Hannah?" she asked abruptly.

He turned at the top of the staircase, the handcuffs dangling from his left wrist. "Why do you want to know?"

"Just curious."

A muscle flicked in his jaw. "She's just a woman I used to date."

"A woman who dumped you?"

"She fell in love with another man. But we're still good friends." Tanner's gaze softened. "Actually, I think it may have worked out the best for both of us."

Maddie swallowed. "It's getting late."

He turned around and headed for the honeymoon suite. Maddie hesitated a moment, her world turning on its axis. When she'd followed Tanner to Abilene, she'd learned that he'd been a member of a wedding party staying at the hotel. The rooms had been reserved by the bride.

And her name had been Hannah Cavanaugh.

At the time, she'd assumed that Tanner had been the groom. Now she wasn't so sure. According to Lauren, this Hannah had dumped him for a man named Cabe. Tanner had told her repeatedly that he was the best man at this wedding, not the groom, despite the impression he'd given her in the bar. But it wasn't until she'd found the wedding rings in his pocket that she'd considered his claim might actually be true. The longer she knew him, the more obvious it became that Tanner Blackburn didn't fit the profile of the Kissing Bandit, despite the similarities in appearance. But if Tanner wasn't the Bandit, who was? His twin brother, perhaps?

Maddie couldn't avoid the truth any longer. There was a very real possibility that she'd made a big mistake.

TANNER WOKE UP WELL BEFORE dawn. He could see Maddie sleeping on the chaise longue, her slender body illuminated by opalescent moonbeams streaming through the window. She'd insisted that he take the bed again, even though he'd offered to trade places.

After they'd returned to the honeymoon suite last night, she'd disappeared into the bathroom to take a bubble bath with her poker winnings. Listening to her splash in the tub had been sheer torture as his imagination had gone into overdrive.

Then she'd allowed him to take a bath, too, hooking the handcuffs around the bar above the soap dish. He'd made his bath a cold one, hoping to cool his enflamed body.

The fragrant scent from the bath beads still lingered in the air this morning. It was probably what had made him dream about sharing a bubble bath with her. Gliding over her wet, sleek body and warming the bathwater with the friction of skin against skin. Unfortunately his dream had little chance of coming true. He was running out of time.

Soon her car would be ready and they'd be back on the road. He doubted Maddie intended to make any other unscheduled stops. It would take less than a day to reach Chicago. Once he straightened out this mix-up, they'd probably never see each other again.

He couldn't let that happen.

At least not until they explored this chemistry between them. After over thirty blind dates with women he'd met because of the Texas mail-order magazine, Tanner knew how rare such chemistry was. Even Hannah, who had sparked his interest for a short time, had never ignited the kind of fire that smoldered between him and Maddie. A fire that promised to ignite into a sensuous blaze if they gave it half a chance.

The sound of the telltale click of Harry's toenails on the hardwood flooring in the hallway made Tanner sit up in bed. Maybe there was a way to give them that chance—if he had a little assistance.

Grateful that Maddie had only shackled his left wrist to the headboard, he slowly opened the top drawer of the nightstand, wincing at the slight creak it made. He glanced at Maddie to make sure she was still sleeping. Then he pulled out a sheet of notepaper and a pen and quickly jotted down a note to Eleanor. He knew he was taking a huge risk, but what did he have to lose?

He signed his name, then folded the note in half, before silently climbing out of bed. He stood up, the hardwood floor cool on his bare feet. If he leaned far enough, he could just reach the doorknob.

Gritting his teeth, he stretched his free arm, his fingers brushing the doorknob. He leaned further, the pressure causing the handcuff to bite into his shackled left wrist. It gave him just enough distance to curl his hand around the knob and crack open the door, letting in a thin shaft of light from the hallway.

A noisy sigh made his breath hitch in his throat.

He looked over his shoulder at Maddie, fervently hoping the hall light and the creak of the door hadn't awakened her.

His heartbeat steadied when he saw that she was still asleep. He stood there in silence for several long moments, just to make sure that she was in a deep slumber. Then he leaned down toward the half-open door. He could see the gray poodle curled up on a rug at the top of the staircase.

"Harry," he called softly. "Come here, boy."

The poodle didn't move.

Tanner whistled low, causing Harry's ears to perk up. The dog scrambled to its feet, then turned and looked toward the open door.

"Come, Harry," Tanner called in a low whisper. "Come on, boy."

Harry hesitated only a moment, then trotted over to the door.

"Good boy," Tanner whispered, scratching the poodle behind his ears. "Good dog."

Harry closed his eyes, enjoying the attention.

Tanner glanced over at Maddie, thankful she was such a sound sleeper. Not the best trait for a bounty hunter, perhaps, but it definitely worked to his advantage.

He held the note up in front of the poodle's face. "See this, Harry?"

Harry cocked his head to one side.

"Give this to Eleanor." He extended his hand,

hoping a dog smart enough to watch CNN was smart enough to obey a simple command. "Take it to Eleanor, boy. She'll give you a treat."

Harry clamped his mouth around the note, then turned and scurried down the hallway, his toenails clicking all the way.

Tanner quietly closed the door, then climbed back into bed. He rubbed his shoulder, the muscle slightly sore from his long stretch toward the door. If his plan worked, it would be well worth the pain.

Now he just had to wait until daybreak to find out.

11

MADDIE STOOD IN FRONT OF a box fan in the corner of Mobleys' repair shop. It provided welcome relief from the humid Kansas morning. Her hair hung in damp, unruly curls around her face. "I don't understand. Eleanor told me that you called right after breakfast and said my car was ready to go."

Mrs. Mobley held a glass of iced tea against one flushed cheek, then the other. "In case you haven't noticed, Eleanor Cutter is a few slices short of a full loaf of bread."

"You mean it's not ready?"

Mrs. Mobley shook her head. "Farming comes first around here, tinkering on cars second. Clayton has to cultivate the north eighty this morning. So your car won't be ready until late afternoon."

"That's no problem," Maddie assured her, realizing she wasn't as disappointed as she should be at the delay. "I can wait." It must be the heat, she thought, plucking at the bodice of her dress. The hot Kansas sun had plastered it to her skin on the walk from Eleanor's house to the Mobleys' garage. Droplets of perspiration rolled between her breasts and strands of her hair stuck to her face. Maybe she should take another cooling bubble bath. Or better yet, spend the day at the air-conditioned beauty salon on main street.

The more distance she kept between herself and Tanner, the better off she'd be.

Especially after what had happened this morning. They'd both slept long past sunrise. When she'd finally awakened, the first thing she'd seen was Tanner asleep in the bed, the crisp white sheet tangled low around his hips. Sometime during the night, he'd taken off his shirt, probably in deference to the heat, giving her the perfect opportunity to leisurely view his powerful chest and broad shoulders. His big hands had bracketed the pillow and she couldn't help remembering how those hands had felt against her skin the night they'd first met.

Maddie mentally shook herself. Why was she letting him get to her this way? Just because of some unfathomable electricity between them? Just because he wasn't like so many other men, who could only feel masculine if she played helpless?

Tanner Blackburn wasn't intimidated by her independence. He didn't sulk when she outwitted him or try to imply that a mere woman had no business being a bounty hunter. He even seemed to enjoy their mental tussles almost as much as their physical ones.

Maddie blinked as a new revelation washed over

her. If he wasn't a felon, Tanner would be the perfect man for her. The kind of man she'd believed could only exist in her fantasies.

"Sorry if I seem a bit cranky." Mrs. Mobley turned and flipped up the fan a notch. "It's this awful heat. Listen, I'll have Clayton drive your car to Eleanor's house as soon he's finished with it. I know you're in a hurry to be on your way. And we'll fill up the gas tank, too. No extra charge."

"Thank you," Maddie said, touched by the small-town generosity. She'd chafed at being stuck in Crab Orchard, anxious to close the case on the Kissing Bandit. Life seemed to stand still here, allowing her too much time to think, too much time to wonder if her single-minded determination had led her down the wrong path.

Now she needed help to find her way back again.

And there was one person who might be able to provide that help—Shayna Walters. Her best friend in boarding school, Shayna had shared Maddie's interest in a criminal justice career. After graduation they'd gone their separate ways, Shayna earning a degree from Cornell while Maddie had gone to Northwestern. But they'd made it a point to keep in touch. Shayna now worked as a data analyst with the Justice Department. She was also the one who had given Maddie a subscription to *Texas Mail-Order Men* as a joke.

Maddie left the Mobleys' garage and headed a few

blocks away to the only telephone booth she'd seen in Crab Orchard. This was a call she couldn't risk making from the Cutter house.

She tugged open the door of the phone booth, then stepped inside. It was like a sauna, the heat intensified at least twenty degrees by the clear panels of the booth.

She picked up the receiver and dialed the operator, charging the call to her home phone number.

"How may I direct your call?" asked an operator with a hint of a southern accent.

"Philadelphia, please. I need the number for Shayna Walters."

A moment later, the connection was made. She swallowed hard, the receiver growing slippery in her grasp. This phone call could change her life.

"Hello?"

"Hi, Shayna."

A moment of silence, then a surprised laugh. "Hey, Maddie, where have you been? I've been trying to reach you for the last week. I met a new guy."

She smiled. Shayna was relentless in her pursuit of men, both in her work and her love life. "I've been out of town on a fugitive apprehension case."

"Cool! Does this mean your dad has finally agreed to let you join the family business?"

"We Griffins are stubborn," Maddie said, "but I think I found a way to convince him I can do the job."

"Ironic, isn't it?" Shayna mused. "Miss Emily's two biggest rule-breakers are now in law enforcement. I track criminals with my computer and you're out in the field."

"Actually, that's the reason I'm calling." Maddie took a deep breath. "I need a favor."

"No problem," Shayna replied. "I still owe you for all the times you covered for me when I was hot and heavy with that guy from Stilton Prep. Remember him?"

"Tall, blond, in love with himself?"

"That's the one. So what can I do for you?" Shayna asked.

"I need all the info you can give me on a guy named Blackburn. Tanner Blackburn."

"Do you have any vital statistics?"

"He's in his late twenties or early thirties, has a sister named Lauren, and currently resides in Dallas, Texas."

"Anything else?"

He's a great kisser. But Maddie didn't want to share that tidbit. Especially if it ended up that the Kissing Bandit had turned her into another dupe. "No, that's about it."

"Okay, give me a minute to key in the information."

"You can do that at home?" Maddie hadn't expected immediate answers. She suddenly wasn't so sure she wanted to find out the truth. But was she more afraid that Tanner really was the Kissing Bandit, or that he wasn't?

"I've got a connection to the main terminal at work. And it looks like I've got something coming up on the screen now."

Maddie's eyes grew hazy and she realized she was holding her breath. She leaned against the hot panel of the phone booth, telling herself to relax.

"Are you looking for anything in particular?" Shayna asked.

"Aliases. Any criminal activities. Marriage records."

"Marriage? Do you want to collar this guy, Maddie, or date him?"

"It's a long story," she hedged.

"Promise you'll tell it to me next time we get together."

"Definitely." She just hoped the story had a happy ending.

"Okay," Shayna announced several minutes later. "The data is in. Here's the scoop on Tanner Blackburn."

"KNOCK, KNOCK." ELEANOR'S voice called through the bedroom door.

Tanner sat up in bed, hastily buttoning his shirt. "Come in."

She walked through the door, Harry prancing in

behind her. "I saw your wife leave a little while ago, so we don't have much time."

"I appreciate your help, Eleanor." Tanner swung his legs over the side of the bed. "Did you bring a hacksaw?"

"No, I brought something even better." She stepped toward the door. "Come in, Leroy."

"Leroy?"

"My nephew," she replied, as a lanky red-haired man walked into the room. "He's a locksmith from Elk City, which is only twenty miles from here."

Leroy looked as if he's spent his life on a horse, his long legs bowed slightly at the knees. He carried a worn attaché case and a friendly smile. "Lucky for you, Aunt Ellie, I don't charge mileage for relatives." Then he looked at Tanner. "So what seems to be the problem?"

"This is a little embarrassing," Tanner said, sliding his left wrist out from under the sheet so they could see the pink handcuffs linking his arm to the wrought-iron headboard. "My wife and I are trying to inject a little excitement into our love life, only we had a fight and now she refuses to turn me loose."

"I usually don't interfere in my guests' lives," Eleanor said, two rosy spots in her withered cheeks. "But it's so obvious that these two belong together. Harry insisted that we help."

"Old Harry must be a matchmaker at heart," Leroy said, reaching down to pet the poodle's head.

Tanner couldn't argue about that. He had a new respect for Harry, and for Eleanor's devotion to him.

Eleanor walked over to the window. "You'd better hurry, Leroy. Maddie could return at any moment."

Leroy knelt down beside the bed to get a closer look at the handcuffs. "I see you're a customer of the Pleasure Chest in Wichita. I haven't seen them in pink before, though."

Eleanor frowned. "How do you know about such places, Leroy? You're not married."

He winked at Tanner. "A friend told me about them, Aunt Ellie."

"Can you unlock them?" Tanner asked, aware that Maddie could walk through the door at any moment.

"Sure." Leroy dug through his case. "The locks on these sex toys aren't sophisticated. I can do it one of two ways. Jimmy the mechanism so it unlocks, or manipulate the mechanism to fit one of the smaller skeleton keys I have in my case."

"What about the original key? Will it still work?"

Leroy shook his head. "If I adjust the mechanism, it won't fit anymore."

Tanner considered this intriguing option. "Is it possible to make the adjustment to all three cuffs? So the new key works, but the old key doesn't."

"No problem," Leroy assured him.

He smiled. "Perfect."

Leroy inserted a narrow metal pick into the lock,

twisting it twice. Then he handed Tanner a slim silver key. "Try it."

Tanner inserted the key into the lock mechanism of the cuff around his wrist. He turned the key, then heard a very satisfying click. The cuff sprung open, freeing his wrist. "It works."

Leroy quickly made the same adjustment to the locks on the other two cuffs. "There you go," he said, packing up his case.

Tanner flexed his wrist, enjoying the freedom. "I don't know how to thank you."

"Twenty-five bucks should about do it. That's my usual rate for a service call."

Tanner looked up at Eleanor. "I'm a little short on cash right now. Could I possibly impose on you to pay the fee, then you can add the charge to our bill?"

Eleanor looked down at the poodle. "What do you think, Harry?"

The tiny dog responded with a shrill bark.

"Harry says that will be fine." Eleanor smiled. "With interest, of course."

"Of course," Tanner replied.

Leroy chuckled. "I've tried to entice Harry to come work for me, but he's loyal to Aunt Ellie. I could probably make a fortune with that mutt."

A low growl emanated from the poodle.

Eleanor scowled. "You know we don't allow that kind of language in this house, Leroy."

"Sorry, Aunt Ellie." He leaned over to pat the top of the dog's head. "Sorry, Harry."

"You're forgiven," Eleanor replied. "Now come downstairs and I'll pack up a box of my special chocolate chunk cookies for you to take home."

"Oh, one more thing," Tanner said, sliding the skeleton key under the mattress. "Can we keep this our little secret? I'm sure once Maddie comes to her senses she'd be terribly embarrassed if she discovered anyone knew that she'd left me stranded in handcuffs."

"Our lips are sealed," Eleanor assured him. "Right, Harry?"

The poodle scampered out of the room.

"Confidentiality is part of my business," Leroy said. "You wouldn't believe some of the emergency calls I get. This is quite tame in comparison."

Tanner waited until they left the room before he pumped his fist in the air. *Freedom.* He stretched his arms over his head as he walked around the honeymoon suite. But he knew he didn't have time to waste. He needed to devise his plan.

He moved to the window and looked over the front lawn of the house. He could see Maddie strolling up the sidewalk. She wore a sleeveless denim dress and a pair of sassy white sandals. She held her hair off her neck with one hand twisted in the dark curls. A heated flush stained her cheeks and her dewy skin glowed in the sunlight.

His body responded instantly.

Although he was now free, escape was the last thing he wanted to do, not when he was a prisoner to his desire for Maddie. He had no intention of leaving her gorgeous clutches.

Especially since he'd caught her staring at him this morning while he'd feigned sleep. Felt her gaze drift over his body. His skin had tingled as if she'd actually been touching him instead of only thinking about it. He'd just been glad the sheet had concealed his body's reaction to her sensual perusal.

Staying might be a risk, since she ultimately wanted to throw him in a jail. But it was a risk he was willing to take. He wanted Maddie Griffin. Wanted her more than he'd wanted a woman in a very long time. And he knew from those two brief, passionate encounters they'd shared that she'd be well worth that risk.

She disappeared from his sight as she ascended the front stoop of the house. He could hear Harry bark, then Eleanor's voice on the porch, introducing her to Leroy. Tanner held his breath, hoping they didn't let anything slip to make Maddie suspicious. He wanted her relaxed and unguarded, completely unaware that the situation had changed.

Now he was the hunter.

12

"I'D LIKE TO HAVE A WORD with you, young lady,"
Eleanor announced as Maddie walked up the porch
steps.

A tall man with a shock of red hair and a devilish
grin on his face tipped his hat as he passed her on the
steps. Harry followed him, nipping at his heels.

"That was my nephew Leroy," Eleanor said, wav-
ing goodbye to him.

Maddie gripped one of the white porch columns,
feeling a little dizzy. She wasn't sure whether to
blame the heat or the information Shayna had given
her about Tanner Blackburn.

He wasn't the Kissing Bandit.

At last, Maddie knew without a doubt what her
heart had been trying to tell her for the past few
days. Shayna had confirmed that Tanner Blackburn
had lived in Dallas, Texas, for the last ten years. That
he was an attorney with the law firm of Collins and
Cooksey, and most importantly, that he'd received a
traffic citation for speeding in Dallas on December
sixteenth. That was the same day the Kissing Bandit
had been arraigned in Chicago.

"Sit down," Eleanor ordered, guiding her toward the wicker rocking chair. "You look like you're about to swoon."

"Is there something you wanted to talk to me about?" Maddie asked, sagging into the rocker. "A problem with the bill?"

Eleanor seated herself in the chair next to her. "No, it's something else."

"Okay," she replied, wondering what she would do about Tanner. Let him go, obviously. Should she offer to drive him back to Dallas? Buy him a plane ticket? Seduce him?

Where had that come from? Maddie took a deep breath, wondering if she was suffering from heatstroke.

"There is a serious problem we need to discuss," Eleanor said primly.

Maddie forced those rogue thoughts of seducing Tanner out of her mind. When she finally admitted she'd made a mistake, he'd probably want to kill her, not kiss her. "What problem?"

"You." Eleanor thrust a platter of fragrant cookies in front of her. "Have a cookie. I want to tell you a story."

Maddie took the cookie, growing more confused by the moment. She glanced up at the house, wondering if Tanner was still asleep. He'd probably want to leave immediately, get back to his regularly scheduled life, and as far away from her as possible.

Maddie glumly bit into the still-warm cookie, its rich flavor melting on her tongue. It did make her feel a little better. "This is delicious."

"Thank you," Eleanor said, reaching for a cookie herself. "I got the recipe from Harry's wife."

Maddie watched the poodle bound up the steps, then curl up on the woven welcome mat in front of the door. "Is his wife a poodle, too?"

"Don't be silly," Eleanor chided. "Dogs can't get married."

Maddie knew she should tread carefully. Eleanor might be a fruitcake, but she was a sweet fruitcake. "Isn't Harry your fiancé?"

"He was." Eleanor breathed a wistful sigh. "In 1950. You should have seen the two of us together. People claimed they could actually feel the air crackle around us."

Maddie took another bite of her cookie, still a little confused. "Was Harry a dog then?"

Eleanor laughed. "Of course not. He was very much a man." Her eyes softened. "In every way."

"So what happened?" Maddie asked gently.

"We had a humdinger of a fight." Eleanor's rocker began to sway slowly back and forth. "He wanted to make up, but I was too stubborn. I insisted that he admit that he was the one in the wrong before I'd give him another chance. He refused, since he was every bit as proud as me. The next day he signed up for the marines. I never saw him again."

Maddie was confused again. "You mean he...died?"

"No, he married an Italian girl. They moved to Indiana after he got out of the service and had five children." Eleanor dabbed at her eyes with a linen handkerchief.

Maddie reached out to squeeze her hand. "I'm sorry, Eleanor."

"So was I," she sniffed, then smiled down at the sleeping poodle, "until Harry came back into my life five years ago. Come here, sweetie, and have a cookie."

Harry opened his eyes, then bounded off the mat and jumped up on her lap. She rewarded him with the rest of her half-eaten cookie.

"Harry's wife found all my old love letters to him after he died," Eleanor continued. "He'd saved them all these years." Her eyes misted. "She mailed them to me, and the same day they showed up in the mailbox, Harry here showed up on my doorstep. I knew it was a sign."

"I'm happy you found each other again," Maddie said, too touched by the story to question Harry's reincarnation. Eleanor had obviously suffered many decades of regret and loneliness.

"Me, too." Eleanor stroked Harry's head. "But Harry and I can't just sit back and watch you and Tanner make the same mistake we did."

"Our situation is a little different," she began.

"Oh, we know you're not really married."

Maddie blinked. "You do?"

Eleanor chuckled. "My dear, this is a town of five hundred people. That charity kidnapping flyer was old news before you even showed up looking for a room. Now, since you told me a completely different story, I'm assuming neither one is true. Am I right?"

"Yes," Maddie replied, feeling guilty and relieved all at the same time. "I'm sorry we lied to you, Eleanor. I didn't see any other way out of my dilemma at the time."

She waved away Maddie's apology. "It doesn't matter now. What matters is that, whatever brought you two together, it's obvious to both Harry and I that you have crackle."

"It's not like that," Maddie assured her.

"Yes, it is." Eleanor's tone brooked no disagreement. "If you've got crackle, it's there, whether you want to admit it or not. You and Tanner have it. Now the only question is, what are you going to do with it?"

"Ignore it until it goes away?" Maddie ventured, not ready to face her own feelings.

"And end up an old woman who talks to a dog?"

Harry barked.

Eleanor smiled down at him, scoring her fingers over his fur. "Yes, my darling, I know you're not *really* a dog, but I'm trying to make a point here."

Maddie reached for another cookie, trying to buy

some time to think. *Crackle.* Maddie had felt it, too. Standing next to Tanner was like standing in a lightning storm. Only she was afraid to get struck.

"Now I'm no expert on men," Eleanor said while Maddie munched on her cookie. "But your Tanner looks like a keeper to me."

"It's a little more complicated than that."

"Piddle. I've seen the way he looks at you. He's yours, dear, if you want him."

"I'll have to think about it," she hedged.

"You do that." Eleanor picked up the platter of cookies and handed them to her. "And please help yourself to more cookies. I've got more here than Harry and I can eat."

"Thank you. I'll take these up to Tanner. I know he'll appreciate them."

"Good plan." Eleanor beamed. "Start with the cookies, then work up to the good stuff."

"Good stuff?"

"Do I have to draw you a picture? Lingerie. A striptease. Breakfast in bed. Women really have all the power in these situations—you just have to know how to use what you've got."

"And what if I don't have it?" Maddie voiced the fear that had nagged at her for years.

Eleanor snorted. "As I said before, I've seen the way that man looks at you. All you have to do is open your heart."

"Thanks again for the cookies," Maddie said, wishing it were that simple.

"They're a dollar apiece," Eleanor called from the rocker. "I'll put it on your bill. But the advice is free."

Maddie let the screen door close behind her. The twinge in her stomach made her wish she hadn't indulged in that third chocolate chunk cookie. Or maybe it was Eleanor's words that were making her feel queasy.

When she reached the honeymoon suite, she stood outside the door for a moment, the platter in one hand and the doorknob in the other. Eleanor was right.

It was time to make a decision.

MADDIE OPENED THE DOOR TO the bedroom and was met by a warm, sultry breeze. The white gauze curtains fluttered at the open windows. She turned toward the bed.

"Hot, isn't it?" Tanner lay stretched on his side, his head propped up on his hand. He wore jeans but no shirt, the sunlight streaming through the window provided a perfect view of his bare chest. Broad, muscular, and covered with a wedge of brown hair that narrowed at his waist.

Hot was definitely the word for it.

She handed him the cookies. "These are from Eleanor."

"Remind me to thank her." He set the platter on

the nightstand, then picked up a cookie and took a bite.

She watched him, her mouth watering. But it wasn't a craving for chocolate chunk cookies that came over her. It was the memory of his kiss, so hot and arousing and electric that her toes curled just thinking about it. She turned and walked toward the window, taking a deep breath to gain control of herself.

"I missed you," he said softly.

She gazed out the window, wishing she didn't like so much about him. Not only the way he looked and kissed, but the tenor of his voice, the cadence of his laugh, the way his smile caused her pulse to quicken.

"Maddie?"

She turned to see him licking cookie crumbs off his fingers. Her knees almost buckled as she watched the slow stroke of his tongue. "Yes?"

"I'd like to take a shower."

She gave a quick nod, then walked over to the bed. She was the one in need of a shower, a cold one at that. But at least while he was in the bathroom she'd have some time to herself, time to figure out exactly what she wanted to do.

She retrieved the key from the chain around her neck, then reached for his cuffed wrist.

But his free hand stopped her, curling around her fingers. "You've got some chocolate on your mouth."

She swallowed. "I'll wash it off."

He leaned toward her. "Let me."

She shook her head, then drew away. But he still held on to her hand. "Please let go of me."

"Are you afraid of me?" he asked, his voice husky.

She didn't feel afraid. Apprehensive was more like it. And incredibly aroused. It occurred to her that since he wasn't the Kissing Bandit, maybe he hadn't been trying to romance his way to freedom. Maybe those kisses and the heat in his eyes were the real thing.

Maybe he wanted her as much as she wanted him.

"Tell me the truth," he said huskily. "Are you afraid?"

She looked into his eyes. "No."

He smiled. "Good." Then he picked up the empty cuff dangling next to him and slapped it around her wrist. "Gotcha."

She blinked in surprise. "What are you doing?"

"Staking my claim."

"This is silly," she said, even as the heat in his gaze uncoiled something deep inside of her. She inserted the handcuff key into the lock. "All I have to do is unlock it...." Her voice trailed off when she realized the key wouldn't turn.

"Your key doesn't work anymore." He leaned back against the pile of pillows.

She jerked on the cuff, but it held fast. She was furious with herself for letting down her guard yet again. And uncertain what she should do next. She knew she wasn't in any danger. A scream would send Eleanor running up here.

Or would it?

Their earlier conversation had made it clear Eleanor believed Tanner and Maddie belonged together.

Her heart raced in her chest. She took a deep breath, trying to remain calm. "I don't know what you're trying to accomplish here, but we can't stay handcuffed to this bed forever."

"Oh, I have a key that works."

"Where did you get a key?" she asked, her mind spinning. Then she threw her key onto the bed. "And why won't this one work anymore?"

"Eleanor has a nephew who's a locksmith," he explained.

"You could have escaped...." The words trailed off as realization washed over her. He didn't look like a man who wanted to run away from her. Just the opposite, in fact. Her mouth went dry as his gaze slid over her body.

"You look so sexy in that dress."

She licked her lips. "Don't do this to me, Tanner."

He leaned up on one elbow. "Do what?"

"I'm not sexy. I don't need to be sexy to do my job."

He stared at her for a long moment. "Why don't you want to believe me? Believe that you're sexy. Believe that I'm not the cad you think I am. Believe that I want you. Only you, Maddie."

Eleanor's words echoed in her mind. *He's yours...if you want him.*

She sucked in a deep breath, trying to gather her scattered wits. "I can't believe Eleanor was in on this."

"It's not like she committed a crime," he said softly. "She thinks I'm your husband."

Maddie didn't know whether to laugh or cry. The little old lady had outfoxed them both. "Eleanor is a lot more savvy than she led us to believe."

Tanner reached over and brushed a tendril of hair off her cheek. "Sit down. You're as pale as that pillowcase."

"I'm fine," she replied, her knees buckling as she sank down onto the mattress.

"I can tell," he said wryly. Then his eyes grew serious. "You're under the mistaken impression that I'm some Casanova, when nothing could be further from the truth. The last woman I dated dumped me for another man. Before that, I was too busy attending PTA meetings and estate closings to have much time for romance. But ever since we met, there's been something between us..." His voice trailed off as he struggled to find the right word.

"Crackle," she whispered. Maddie felt it stronger than ever now. It hovered around them and between them, making time stand still.

He moved closer to her. "You feel it, too?"

She tensed, all of her senses heightened by his nearness. "This has never happened to me before."

"That makes two of us."

"I think I owe you an apology," she began, as he closed the distance between them.

"I don't want an apology," he murmured, his lips brushing against her mouth. "I want you."

_____ 13 _____

MADDIE CLOSED HER EYES AS he captured her small moan with his kiss, his free hand cupping the back of her head. She leaned into him as he deepened the kiss, his tongue seeking entrance into her mouth. She surrendered with another moan, placing her hands on his powerful chest. The muscles flexed beneath her fingertips.

Tanner Blackburn kissed her like no man ever had before—tenderly, reverently, hungrily. Maddie knew then it was too late to turn back. She didn't want to retreat. No more doubts. No more second thoughts. She'd wanted the Kissing Bandit and gone after him with single-minded determination.

She wanted Tanner more.

He lifted his head, his breathing fast and unsteady. "Do you want me to let you go?"

Her gaze fell to the handcuffs linking them together. The third cuff lay loose on the mattress, no longer hooked around the headboard. They could move away from the bed, but not from each other.

"No," she said at last. *Never.*

A smile played on his mouth. "Good. Because

you're my prisoner. You have to do whatever I ask."
His voice was low and husky. So sexy it almost made
her melt into the sheets.

"Then ask."

Desire flared in his eyes. "The first thing I want
you to do is take off your shoes."

She kicked off her sandals and let them clatter to
the floor. "Now what?"

"Touch me."

She swallowed. "Where?"

He leaned back against the pillows. "Anywhere
you want."

Maddie let her gaze drift from his face to his chest
to the sheet at his waist. She'd imagined herself
touching him countless times during the past few
days. Now she didn't know where to start.

She tentatively reached out her unfettered hand
and lightly ruffled her fingers over the dark hair on
his chest. It surprised her how soft it was, in contrast
to the hard, contoured muscles beneath. She molded
her palm to the washboard ripples of his stomach.
Shayna had told her that Tanner Blackburn had been
a champion swimmer in high school. He still had the
body of a well-conditioned athlete.

Her fingers strayed upward, whirling around one
flat nipple. His sharp intake of breath told her how
much he liked the sensation. Emboldened by a new-
found feminine power, Maddie expanded her explo-
ration of his body. Her fingers traced the firm arcs of

his biceps and trailed up over his solid shoulders, then swept back down his chest to his navel.

His breathing quickened as her hand dipped beneath the waistband of his jeans.

"Stop," he said, snatching her wrist before she could explore any further. But she'd gone just far enough to discover his arousal. The knowledge made her hesitate. Could she really trust him?

He tipped up her chin with his finger. "Yes. You can trust me."

She blinked. "How did you know?"

"Because it's almost like I can see into your soul. I know that sounds corny, but it's true." He let go of her chin, his knuckle now stroking her cheek. "I've seen you watching me, Maddie. Just like I've been watching you. Only there's been doubt in your eyes. I can see it there now."

She reached out her hand, grazing her palm over the rough whiskers on his jaw. "I want to trust you."

"And I want to prove to you that you can."

Before she knew what was happening, Tanner hooked the empty cuff around her free wrist. Then he pulled a key from under the mattress and unlocked the cuff around his own wrist.

A bolt of panic surged through her. "What are you doing?"

"Proving that you can trust me." He hooked his now empty cuff around the headboard. Then he swung his legs over the side of the bed and rose to his feet.

Maddie waited for him to run out the door. He had her exactly where he wanted her, completely at his mercy.

He folded his arms across his bare chest. "Now you're in charge."

"Hardly," she said, trying to sound unfazed by this turn of events. She lay on the bed, her handcuffed wrists stretched over her head and the third cuff chained to the headboard. She couldn't believe she'd been foolish enough to let him put her in this position.

"I mean it." He walked over to the door and opened it. "I could walk out of here right now and you'd never see me again."

She swallowed. "So why don't you?"

He closed the door. "Because I'd rather be here with you. If you want me."

Her doubts battled with her desire. But it wasn't a fair fight. Not with Tanner standing before her like a Greek god. She simply didn't want to fight these feelings anymore. "I want you."

He walked over to the bed. "May I kiss you?"

She nodded, wondering why he'd even bothered to ask when she was helpless to stop him.

Tanner put one knee on the bed as he leaned down to kiss her lips, briefly, chastely. Then he straightened. "Now what?"

She wrinkled her brow. "I don't understand."

"You're in charge, Maddie," he said softly. "What do you want me to do?"

And, in that moment, she understood. He'd caught her in his snare, then surrendered. She was his captive—but he was treating her like his captor. He would follow her every command though she was helpless before him. His behavior just reiterated the fact that Tanner Blackburn was a special man.

A man she could trust.

"Kiss me again," she said, her voice a little shaky from the revelation.

He obeyed her order without hesitation, this kiss full of passion and heat and promise. His body stretched beside hers, his hands gently kneading her shoulders. "You are so beautiful," he whispered, as his lips burned a trail down her throat.

And for the first time in her life, she truly felt beautiful. She closed her eyes as his lips skimmed her collarbone then moved to the V of her sundress. He began to slide the strap of her sundress over her shoulder, then put it back again, his gaze lifting to meet hers.

"Yes," she said, before he even asked the question. She'd been able to read it in his eyes, just as he'd done to her.

He hooked his fingers under the strap of her sundress and slowly pulled it off one shoulder, then he did the same with the other strap. Her breathing quickened as the bodice of her sundress gaped open, revealing the tops of her breasts and the red lace of her strapless bra.

"Oh, Maddie," he breathed, heat flaring in his eyes.

"Take if off," she whispered huskily, her arms straining above her head. She wanted to feel the weight of his body against her own.

He pulled the sundress down to her waist, then unhooked the front clasp of her bra. It fell away, and he dipped his head to kiss her right nipple.

She moaned softly as his lips teased and tasted, driving her half mad. She wanted to taste him, too. To touch him. But the handcuffs made it impossible.

"Tanner," she cried, straining against the restraint.

He lifted his head to look up at her. "What do you want, Maddie? Just tell me what you want."

"More," she gasped, unable to be more specific. She wanted Tanner. All of him. Forever.

He smiled, then leaned down to lavish his attention on her other breast, his body still not coming into contact with hers. She closed her eyes and let the exquisite sensations carry her to another plane. Then she felt his hands on the dress bunched at her waist.

She opened her eyes to see him looking expectantly at her. "Yes," she said, realizing he'd meant what he said. He was leaving her in control, letting her make every call. She found it incredibly erotic.

He shimmied the sundress over her hips, revealing the red lace panties underneath. Then he pulled the dress off of her completely and tossed it onto the floor, his gaze never leaving her body.

"Now it's your turn," she ordered, feeling emboldened by her power.

He rose off the bed, then unzipped the fly of his jeans. He pulled them off and tossed them on top of her dress. Then his hands went to the waistband of his blue cotton boxer shorts. He hesitated, waiting for her to direct him.

She licked her lips. "Do it."

Her eyes widened as the boxer shorts fell away. He was more magnificent than she'd ever imagined. Then he was beside her on the bed again, his mouth hovering over hers.

She lifted her head far enough to capture his lips and heard the deep rumble of a groan in his chest. His hard body pressed against hers, and she could feel the evidence of his desire. Then he lifted his head and looked into her eyes.

"Maddie." His voice slid over her like warm honey. "I want..."

"What do you want?" she asked. "Tell me."

"I want you to touch me."

She nodded, then waited impatiently as he found the key to the handcuffs. In another moment, she was free. He set the key on the desk, then pulled out the box of condoms and she heard the rip of foil. The next moment, he was in her arms again. She pulled him on top of her, relishing the weight of his body.

He groaned as she arched against him, then he found her lips and kissed her deeply. His tongue delved inside her mouth, meeting hers in a sensual mating dance. Maddie's hands never stopped moving, touching him everywhere, inflaming him.

Soon they were both hovering on the brink of desperation, their kisses as fervent and heated as their bodies. His palm found her breast, his fingers plucking and stroking until she cried out his name. Then his hand slid down her waist and tangled in her panties. She heard the rip of lace and then she was completely naked beneath him.

Maddie shifted her body until they fit together, molding to each other in perfect harmony. He kissed her, his mouth teasing and tantalizing her, making sensual promises that heightened her need.

His body hovered over her until she issued an invitation by arching up to meet him halfway. He joined her in one swift movement, making them both moan into each other's mouth. Then he began to move, slowly, rhythmically, and the crackle sizzled between them.

It was almost more than she could stand. Maddie felt her climax building inside of her, powerless to stop it even if she wanted to, until it finally exploded in one long shower of sparks and light and ecstasy.

She heard him gasp her name, his hard body rocking into hers one final time.

When she could finally breathe again, Tanner lay boneless on top of her, his head pillowed on her breasts.

She sifted her fingers through his hair, her eyes misting at how close she'd come to never knowing him, knowing this. She might have lost her dream of capturing the Kissing Bandit, but she'd found someone she hadn't dared to even dream about. The love of her life.

"HUNGRY?" TANNER ASKED, holding Maddie in his arms as a cooling breeze from the open window caressed their bodies. It was long past midnight and they'd finally sated each other, putting a serious dent into the box of condoms. But somehow he knew he'd never have enough of her.

"No, I'm fine," Maddie murmured, her body curled into his. "Just thinking."

"About what?"

"The Kissing Bandit." She placed one hand on his chest. "I know it's not you. I called a friend today who works at the Justice Department and she told me your story checks out."

"So I'm innocent?" he asked, a teasing note in his voice.

"I wouldn't say that." She leaned up to kiss him. "But you're off my list of suspects. I suppose it's possible you could have invented this elaborate cover to hide your illegal activities, but my instincts tell me differently."

"I like your instincts," he said, running his hand over her naked hip. "But then I like everything about you."

"The thing that bothers me the most is the mug shot," she mused. "It looks so much like you."

His fingers lightly traced figure eights on her thigh. "Do you have it with you?"

She shook her head. "When I saw your picture in the *Texas Mail-Order Men* magazine, I assumed you'd altered your hair color and your appearance, so the mug shot would be outdated anyway."

He could hear the tension in her voice. "Tell me what you're thinking."

She hesitated a moment. "Is it possible the real Kissing Bandit could be related to you?"

He sighed. "Ronnie."

"That's the twin brother Lauren mentioned on the phone?"

He nodded. "Fraternal not identical, but people still had trouble telling us apart when we were younger."

"What's Ronnie like?"

"We're not close." Tanner thought about his brother's life—the parade of women, the bad loans, the job hopping and nomadic lifestyle. "But if you want to know if he fits the profile of a man who uses women and is always in need of cash, I'm afraid the answer is yes."

"And he's been out of the country?"

Tanner nodded. "For the last five months."

"So that's why no one could find him." Maddie stared up at the ceiling, her face pensive.

Tanner leaned up on his elbow, brushing a stray curl off her cheek. "Why is finding the Kissing Bandit so important to you?"

She turned on her side to face him, tangling one slender leg between his knees. "The Griffin Bail Enforcement Agency is the best in Chicago, maybe the country. My father prides himself on his tracking skills. I can remember when I was home on holidays from boarding school, hearing him tell these wonderful stories about his cases. Ben and Tate and I all dreamed about becoming a bounty hunter just like him."

Tanner could hear the wistfulness in her voice. And the pain.

"Their dreams came true," she continued, "but Dad refused to give me a chance. Even after I got my degree and wanted to take a few easy cases to prove myself, my brothers would always interfere."

"So you decided to go after a hard case?"

She nodded. "The Kissing Bandit stole my father's fiancée out from under him. So now it's become a family vendetta to find him, only Dad and my brothers haven't had any luck. I thought if I found him, I'd finally prove to my dad that I belonged in the family business." Her voice caught. "That they needed me."

Tanner drew her into his arms. "I need you."

She kissed him, then looked up into his eyes. "What do you want to do about your brother?"

His heart contracted. "You're leaving the decision up to me?"

"I think that's only fair, since I never should have nabbed you in the first place."

"I'm glad you did," he said huskily. Then sighed. "I just can't believe that Ronnie is the Kissing Bandit. I know he fits the description, both in appearance and behavior, but I always just thought he was a bum, not a criminal."

"Has he ever been married? Or engaged?"

Tanner shook his head. "Not that I know of—which doesn't mean he's innocent." He reached for her hand. "If my brother really is the Kissing Bandit, then he can't go on breaking the law. I'm duty bound as an officer of the court, if nothing else, to see him brought to justice. But he's still my brother. I want to make sure he gets good legal counsel, and that all the women he's taken money from are reimbursed somehow."

Maddie reached up to kiss him. "Have I told you lately how glad I am that I caught you?"

He smiled. "No, but you can show me instead."

She did, seducing him with fevered kisses and

bold caresses until they both forgot everything except each other. They made slow, sweet love, this time melding their hearts and souls, as well as their bodies. Then they just held on to each other.

"There's one thing I haven't told you about Ronnie," he said into the darkness. His mind still couldn't reconcile the fact that his own brother might be a criminal, might be capable of treating women so cruelly.

Maddie's soft breath warmed his neck. "What's that?"

"Just for kicks, he likes to pretend to be me."

14

MADDIE WOKE UP SLOWLY the next morning, the sun high in the sky by the time she finally opened her eyes. She straightened her legs, wincing slightly at the tender muscles on her body. The aftereffects of a long, passionate night. She and Tanner had eaten oranges and bananas from the fruit bowl sometime after two in the morning, playing silly games with the fruit that had evolved into passionate lovemaking.

She turned lazily onto her back, stretching like a satisfied cat. Then she noticed she was alone in bed. She sat up, craning her head toward the bathroom. "Tanner?"

No answer.

Then she saw the note on his pillow. With shaking fingers, she picked it up. The writing was neat and even. The content made her heart plummet to her toes.

Maddie,
I want to make your dream come true. I'm going to find the Kissing Bandit and bring him back to you. Wait for me.

Yours always,
Tanner

"I don't believe it." The big, dumb, lovable jerk had decided to jump in and do her job for her. Just like her father and brothers. Probably with the same misguided notion of protecting her. Didn't he realize that bringing in a fugitive was both dangerous and tricky? Even if that fugitive was his brother?

Maddie got up and threw her clothes on, hoping she could catch Tanner before he left town. No doubt he was headed for Hominy, Iowa, since that's where Lauren had said Ronnie had gone. Crab Orchard didn't have a bus or train terminal, so Tanner probably planned to hitch a ride with someone.

Then another thought occurred to her. She looked out her window, expecting to see her Toyota Camry parked by the curb. It wasn't there.

She flew out the bedroom door and hurried down the staircase. "Eleanor?"

"I'm right here." Eleanor walked out of the kitchen, still drying a platter with the dish towel in her hands.

"Did Clayton Mobley deliver my car last night?"

"Yes. He stopped in for a moment to tell me he'd left the keys on the dashboard. I would have given you the message last night but I didn't want to disturb you."

"Have you seen Tanner this morning?" Maddie asked, fearing the worst.

Eleanor smiled. "He ordered breakfast for you shortly before he went out. Pancakes, eggs, sausage and some of my special honey oat muffins. It's almost ready."

Even if she had time to eat, it would be impossible. Her stomach was twisted into a tight knot. "What time did he leave?"

Eleanor shrugged. "I'd say about an hour ago."

And thanks to the Mobleys he had a full tank of gas.

Maddie wouldn't let herself think the worst. That she'd been duped by the Kissing Bandit. That he'd made love to her, then stolen her car, leaving her high and dry.

Tanner Blackburn wasn't the Kissing Bandit. She knew it in her bones. He was a decent, honorable man who was about to find himself way in over his head. And since she happened to be very fond of that head, as well as the rest of his body, it was up to her to figure out a way to rescue him.

THE TOWN OF HOMINY, IOWA, had never held much excitement for Tanner. He'd spent a few summers here when he was a teenager, along with his brother Ronnie and cousin Cabe, doing odd jobs for his grandmother. She had been a prickly woman with a fondness for crocheting and Lawrence Welk.

He yawned as he drove down the highway, half wishing he'd stayed in bed with Maddie instead of embarking on his romantic crusade. But then he remembered the pain in her voice when she spoke of her lost dream and he was glad he'd made the five-hour trip. The job ahead of him wouldn't be easy, but it was something he had to do.

If he discovered Ronnie really was the Kissing Bandit, then he was going to make his brother accountable for his crimes. And he'd make sure Maddie got credit for bringing him to justice.

An early wedding present.

"Hold on, Blackburn," he said, as he turned onto the blacktop road leading into Hominy. "You're getting way ahead of yourself."

He and Maddie hadn't even discussed dating, much less marriage. He hadn't told her he loved her, preferring to communicate his feelings with his hands and his body.

His groin tightened just thinking about their night together. He couldn't wait to get back to her. Once this Kissing Bandit business was settled, they could focus their concentration on each other. See if their relationship had potential outside a pair of handcuffs.

A chorus of barking dogs welcomed him into the sleepy hamlet. He hadn't been to Hominy in over ten years, but it was almost as if time had stood still. He saw the same café, grocery store, three bars, and assorted seed and grain dealerships lining both sides of the street. The only new business was a beauty salon called *Wigged Out*. A montage of wigs and toupees was displayed in the front window.

He drove by the park, where a group of young children were busy painting the bandstand. Several new seedlings had been planted among the towering oaks.

His grandmother's place looked the same, too. A simple two-story white house with crisp black shutters. The front porch was bordered by flowering spirea bushes, their big white blossoms emitting a sweet scent as he climbed the porch steps.

This was Cabe's house now, but he knew his cousin wouldn't mind if he camped out here while he searched for Ronnie. Tanner ran his hand along the bottom of the windowsill, finding a splinter before his fingers connected with a metal key. His grandmother had always kept a spare house key taped under the front windowsill. It seemed odd, since she'd never locked her doors. After her death, he'd contacted the sheriff to close up the house and lock all the doors and windows. Fortunately, he'd forgotten to mention the key.

But before he could retrieve it, the front door opened. "Hey, Tanner, this is a surprise."

He straightened and looked into the face of his cousin. "Cabe?"

"Come on in." Cabe waved him inside.

"Where's Hannah?" Tanner stepped into the living room, noting that the old place even smelled the same. A curious mix of lavender and mothballs. He half expected his stout grandmother to step out of the kitchen, wiping her hands on her apron.

"She's not here at the moment." Cabe sat down in one of the worn armchairs, adorned by their grandmother's hand-crocheted antimacassars. "What are you doing in Hominy?"

Tanner was a little surprised Cabe was still speaking to him, since he'd been AWOL from his wedding. He looked around the house, noting the dust-covers on the rest of the furniture and the drapes pulled over the window. Hardly a romantic place for a honeymoon. But it seemed perfect for a hideout.

He centered his gaze on Cabe. "I'm looking for the Kissing Bandit."

Cabe propped his feet on the ottoman. "Has a nice ring to it, doesn't it?"

Tanner stared at him as everything fell into place. Cabe's whirlwind courtship with Hannah. His mysterious past. His lack of interest in inviting any of his friends or other family members to the wedding.

Hannah was a wealthy woman. Tanner had even given her advice when the distribution of her grandfather's sizable estate had been challenged in court. Cabe had expressed keen interest in the case. But had his real interest been in the estate's main beneficiary?

Tanner rubbed one hand over his jaw, wondering how he could have been so stupid. Hannah had called him at home last Saturday. Lauren had said she'd sounded upset. Had Hannah been searching for the wedding rings...or her bridegroom?

A wave of relief rolled through him that Ronnie might not be guilty after all. But he had to be sure. "You stood Hannah up at the altar."

"She'll get over it." Cabe leaned back in his chair. "They always do. I hated to give up all that lovely money, especially since she hadn't even asked me to sign a prenuptial."

No doubt Tanner's early morning phone call about being harassed by a crazed bounty hunter had scared Cabe off. He'd realized the authorities were looking for him, so he'd hightailed it out of town, leaving both his bride and his best man stranded.

Tanner's hands squeezed the arms of the chair as anger simmered inside of him. Hannah was a nice woman who didn't deserve such callous treatment. And Maddie. Maddie had made an honest mistake. She didn't deserve to lose the dream of her lifetime because his slick cousin had pulled another disappearing act.

His eyes narrowed. "Do you have any idea how much I want to knock that grin right off you face?"

Cabe held up both hands. "Hey, we're family, remember?"

"How could you do this to Hannah? And to me? What if I had really been in love with her?"

Cabe shook his head. "Hannah was all wrong for

you. Bossy as hell. And could you really imagine yourself getting married in a barn?"

No, he couldn't. He couldn't imagine himself with any woman except Maddie. In a sense, he owed Cabe. If the jerk hadn't stolen Hannah from him, Tanner and Maddie might never have met.

"But if you really want her back," Cabe continued. "Hannah is still free. I took off as soon as I got your phone call." He smiled, confirming Tanner's suspicions. "Thanks for the heads up. I hope the creep didn't give you too much trouble."

"I survived." *And fell in love.*

Cabe sighed. "I took it as a sign that my Kissing Bandit days are over. That was a damn close call."

Tanner folded his arms across his chest. "Is that why you're here?"

Cabe nodded. "Laying low until the heat is off."

His cousin might share the same physical features as Tanner and his brother, but that's where the resemblance ended. Cabe was a lowlife who deserved to pay for his crimes.

"What made you do it?" Tanner asked, wondering if he'd ever really known his cousin. "What exactly was the thrill of breaking all those women's hearts?"

Cabe shrugged. "You don't understand. I never wanted to hurt anyone. It started with Danielle. Do you remember her?"

Tanner shook his head.

"She was one of those luscious farm girls they grow here in Hominy. I met her the last summer I spent with Grandma when I was nineteen. One Saturday night Danielle and I were at the movies and she left to go get some popcorn. Her purse was right there and I happened to see her cash card."

"You snooped through her purse?"

"I was looking for a stick of gum." Cabe settled back in his chair. "Anyway, I knew the password for her cash card because Danielle believed we shouldn't have any secrets between us. So I pocketed the card, just as a joke, to see if she'd notice."

"And did she?"

"I don't know. She broke up with me that night." A muscle flicked in Cabe's jaw. "So I went to the dog races in Council Bluffs the next day to cheer myself up. When I ran out of cash, I decided to borrow some money from Danielle's account. I figured she owed me at least that much for breaking my heart."

"And the rest is history."

"Hell, Tanner, it's just too damn easy. Over half the women I pilfer money from never even report me to the cops, so they must not miss the money too much."

"Or else they were too embarrassed to admit they'd been taken in by a slick con artist."

"Hey, watch your language. I'm still your cousin."

"Don't remind me."

Cabe leaned forward in the chair. "So will you represent me?"

Tanner blinked. "What?"

"I have several assets, like this house for instance, that I'd like to liquidate. Since it's getting a little too hot for me in the States, I need to go international. I was hoping you could handle the business end here for me."

He couldn't believe his arrogance. "Sorry, you'll have to find another lawyer. I have a conflict of interest." *And her name is Maddie.*

"Because we're related?"

"No, because I plan to turn you over to the bounty hunter who nabbed me."

Cabe laughed. "How exactly do you plan to do that? Do you honestly think I'll go without putting up a fight?"

Tanner stood up, ready to take out his anger on Cabe's smug face. "You can try it."

"Okay." Cabe rose, then reached under his T-shirt and pulled out a 9mm gun from his waistband. "I win."

15

"ARE YOU READY TO ORDER?"

Maddie sat at a booth in the Perk Up Café, holding a blue paper menu in her hands. She'd arrived in Hominy an hour ago, tired and frustrated that her flight from Wichita to Des Moines had been delayed by a thunderstorm. No doubt Tanner was already here. Now she just had to find him.

Maddie set down the menu. "I'll have a cup of coffee and a grilled cheese sandwich, please."

The waitress jotted the order down on her notepad. "We have a special on coconut cream pie today. Only ninety-nine cents a slice."

Maddie pulled a twenty-dollar bill out of her purse and slid it across the table. "If I skip the pie and just want some answers, will this be enough to cover it?"

The waitress looked around the empty café. Then she shrugged her thin shoulders and slid into the booth across from Maddie. "Depends what you want to know. Are you from the liquor commission?"

"No, I work solo." She leaned forward. "I want to know if you've seen a man in town today."

The waitress laughed. "More like a hundred men. The rain brings all the farmers in from the fields."

"This man isn't a farmer and he isn't from around here. He's tall, over six feet, with dark hair and sky-blue eyes. A dimple in his chin when he smiles. Late twenties. With a Texas drawl."

"You must be talking about Tanner Blackburn."

Maddie's heart skipped a beat. "That's him."

The waitress smiled. "He's a charmer, isn't he? Only Tanner doesn't have a Texas twang. And I should know since he's been here every day for lunch for the past week."

Maddie blinked. "That's impossible."

"He inherited Olive White's house," the waitress said, as if she hadn't heard her. "Olive used to belong to the same bridge club as my aunt Willa. Everybody assumed Mr. Blackburn would sell the house, but it looks to me like he's here to stay awhile."

"How do you know that?" Maddie asked, her mind spinning.

The waitress shrugged. "Aunt Willa took one of her apple cakes over as a housewarming gift. She really just went there to snoop, but that's the polite way of doing it around here."

"And what did she find out?"

"Mr. Blackburn told her he's ready to settle down,

which, naturally, made all the old ladies with single granddaughters toddle over there with food offerings."

Maddie's pulse quickened. The Kissing Bandit's typical m.o. was to charm all the women in his vicinity. What better way to set a trap for an unwitting victim than to play the part of the eligible bachelor? "Sounds like he's quite the catch."

"He's a little too slick for me," she replied. "You know the type—perfect hair, perfect clothes, perfect lines—and just as nosy as all the old ladies."

"In what way?"

"He wanted the scoop on one of the widows in town. Celia Dunham. She was part of the cake brigade, although she hasn't even hit fifty yet. Too old for him, of course, but you wouldn't know it from the way his eyes lit up when he heard about all the irrigated farm ground she owns."

Maddie didn't need to hear any more. It sounded like the Kissing Bandit was on the prowl again.

The waitress stood up. "That's about all I can tell you."

"Can you answer just one more question?"

"Sure. Then I'd better get your order started."

"Where is Olive White's house?"

"Just past the park about three blocks. White house with black shutters. Big fir tree in the front yard. There's a key under the front windowsill in case the door is locked."

If Maddie could nab the Kissing Bandit tonight, she'd be able to deliver him in Chicago before the deadline. Dread filled her at taking down Tanner's own brother. She just hoped Tanner didn't try to interfere.

Maddie formulated a plan while she ate her grilled cheese sandwich. By the time she'd wiped the last crumb from her mouth and drained her cup of coffee, she knew what to do.

"Anything else?" the waitress asked, approaching the table.

Maddie smiled up at her. "I believe I'll have some pie after all."

"SPEAKING AS AN ATTORNEY," Tanner said, his eyes trained on the gun in Cabe's hand. "I should advise you that holding someone at gunpoint is not a good idea."

"Sit down," Cabe ordered, moving a step closer to him.

Tanner slowly lowered himself into the chair. "It's time to give it up, Cabe. You've had a good run, but now it's over."

"I agree." Cabe moved toward the credenza, never taking his eyes or the gun off of Tanner. "I'm done with playing the Kissing Bandit, just like I told you. But I intend to retire in style, in someplace like Rio or Bali."

"That might be a possibility," Tanner said, his

gaze scanning the room for some kind of weapon, "in five to ten years."

Cabe snorted. "That is so typical. Mr. Follow-the-rules. But tell me, Tanner, where exactly has it gotten you? Your life is a snore. Women leave you at the wink of an eye. You're living proof that nice guys finish dead last."

Tanner smiled. "Then why are you the one who is sweating?"

Cabe ripped one hand through his hair. "Because everything is falling apart! First, I find out some bounty hunter is on my trail. Then you come along playing Dudley Do-Right. I need a break."

"Turn yourself in. I'll contact a good criminal attorney. Maybe he can cut you a deal." Tanner inched forward in the chair. If he could reach the coffee table, he might be able to use it as a shield, then make a break for the back door.

"Don't move," Cabe barked. "I don't stake my life on maybes. And you won't be calling anyone until I'm long gone."

He reached behind him and jerked open the top drawer of the credenza. It fell to the floor, spilling several spools of thread, buttons, crochet needles and a ball of variegated yarn.

Tanner tensed as Cabe picked up the yarn and advanced toward him. As long as that gun was pointed toward his chest, he couldn't make a move. "What are you planning to do?"

"First, I'm going to tie you up." Cabe moved beside the chair. He unwound the yarn, letting the ball fall to the polished hardwood floor and roll away from him. Then he began winding the yarn around Tanner's chest and the chair, building so many layers that it was soon as strong as rope.

"There," Cabe said, stepping back to admire his handiwork. "That's much better."

"Speak for yourself," Tanner muttered.

Cabe tugged the wedding ring off of Tanner's finger. "I don't want to forget this. It's worth a lot of money." Then he took the car keys out of Tanner's shirt pocket. "You don't mind if I borrow your car, do you?"

The doorbell rang before Tanner could reply.

"Shit," Cabe muttered, pocketing his gun. He walked over to the window and pulled the lace curtain aside to peek out onto the porch. Then he smiled. "False alarm. It's just another one of Grandma's cronies come to welcome me to Hominy."

He walked toward the door as the doorbell rang again. But before he opened it, he turned toward Tanner. "Don't say a word or the old lady pays the price."

Tanner watched as Cabe opened the front door. He couldn't see anything from his vantage point in the living room. But he could hear the old woman greet Cabe.

Only it wasn't an old woman.

It was Maddie.

MADDIE STOOD ON THE FRONT porch, a large basket in her hands. The cheap gray wig made her scalp itch and the drugstore reading glasses sitting on the end of her nose made her vision a little blurry. But she could see well enough to identify the man who opened the door.

It was the Kissing Bandit. An identical match to the man she'd seen in the mug shot photo. Now that she saw him in person, she wondered how she could ever have mistaken Tanner for the man. There were similarities. Both had the same shade of blue eyes, although this man's gaze was cold and calculating. His jaw was a little leaner, but he was the same height. And his hair color was still blond. Obviously the guy was cocky enough to believe he'd never get caught, so he hadn't bothered to change his appearance since the mug shot.

"Hello," he said, stepping out onto the porch and closing the door behind him. "I'm Tanner Blackburn."

"Hello, Mr. Blackburn." She gave him a wide smile. "I can't tell you what a pleasure it is to finally meet you. I've heard so much about you."

He chuckled. "Grandma tended to exaggerate."

"Oh, I'm sure all the tales I heard were true."

He glanced over his shoulder. "I'd like to invite

you in, ma'am, but I'm afraid you've caught me in the middle of a rather messy project."

"Oh, I can't stay," she assured him. "I'm in the middle of a big project myself. I just wanted to stop by and give you a little something to show you how glad I am you're here."

He leaned toward her basket and sniffed. "What have you got in there?"

She smiled. "There's only one way to find out. Now, close your eyes and hold out your hands. I want to give you a big surprise."

He laughed as he stretched his hands out in front of him.

"No peeking," Maddie admonished, reaching into the basket.

He squeezed his eyes shut. "I can't see a thing."

"Good." She slapped a pair of steel handcuffs on both his wrists.

His eyes flew open. "What the hell?"

Maddie pulled a coconut cream pie out of the basket, balancing it on one hand. "I suggest you not move a muscle. My pie has a special ingredient— pepper spray. I guarantee you won't like the way it tastes or the way it makes your eyes burn."

He gulped. "Okay."

With her free hand, she patted him down, finding the gun half-hidden in the waistband of his pants. "What do we have here?"

"Be careful with that," he admonished, as she dangled it in front of him. "It's loaded."

"Kneel down," she ordered, motioning toward the floor.

After he fell to his knees, she pulled a pair of leg shackles from her basket and bound his ankles.

"Is that really necessary?" he asked.

"It's for your own protection," she said, pulling off the wig and fluffing out her hair. "I'd hate to have to shoot you with your own gun if you tried to run."

He scowled up at her. "Who the hell are you?"

She smiled. "Maddie Griffin, with the Griffin Bail Enforcement Agency. You missed your court appearance in Chicago."

"A woman," he muttered. "I got taken down by a woman."

"I call it poetic justice."

A loud crash sounded from inside the house. Maddie reached into the basket for her stun gun. "Who's in there?"

"Tanner Blackburn, the *real* Kissing Bandit." Hope sparked in his eyes. "My name is Cabe White and I've been held hostage by this creep. I'd just captured him when you rang the doorbell. I mean it, lady, you've nabbed the wrong man. He's the crook."

"Shut up," Maddie said, pulling a roll of duct tape out of her basket. She tore off a piece, then placed it over Cabe's eyes. "There, that should keep you from trying to wander off."

Then she got up and walked cautiously toward the front door. Her knees buckled when she saw Tanner lying on the floor inside, bound to a chair. She ran over to him, running her hands over his body to make certain Cabe hadn't shot him.

"I'm all right," he told her gruffly. "I tipped the chair over to distract Cabe. I thought you were in trouble."

She scattered kisses over his face and neck. "I'm fine. And your cousin Cabe is in custody."

"Are you completely crazy coming here by yourself? Cabe has a gun. He could have killed you!"

"I took his gun away," she said, kneeling beside him. Her heart still raced at the danger he'd been in. "Right after I handcuffed him."

His eyes narrowed. "Please tell me you didn't kiss him."

"No, I've sworn off that method of apprehension." She grabbed hold of the back of the chair and pushed it upright. "Too dangerous."

"Good. Now untie me."

She knelt down on the floor in front of him. "Not until you tell me why I woke up alone this morning."

"Because I didn't want you coming here with your pink handcuffs and your lavender business cards trying to nab the Kissing Bandit. A man can do crazy things when he's desperate. Cabe is proof of that."

"So you were trying to protect me?"

"Damn straight."

She rose to her feet. "That's what I thought."

His eyes softened as he looked up at her. "You were supposed to wait for me in Crab Orchard."

"Wait for you? When you'd just pulled the classic Kissing Bandit move of loving and leaving? You even stole my car!"

"I *borrowed* your car." His brow furrowed. "You can't still believe *I'm* the Kissing Bandit."

"You fit the m.o.," she said huskily. "You made me fall in love with you."

The dimple flashed in his chin. "You're in love with me?"

"Yes." She leaned down to kiss him. "But I can't think about that until I get your cousin into custody. And I have less than forty-eight hours to do it."

"I'll drive. Cabe has the keys in his pocket." He nodded toward the credenza. "There should be a pair of scissors in one of those drawers. As soon as you cut me loose, we can go."

Maddie hesitated. "I don't think so."

"What do you mean?"

"I've got to do this on my own, Tanner."

"Cabe is too dangerous. And he's determined not to go to prison."

"I can handle him."

Tanner looked at her, worry clouding his eyes. "Maddie, this is ridiculous. I'm going with you and that's final."

She walked to the door. "I promise to call the sheriff in a couple of hours, as soon as I'm far enough away from Hominy. He can come out here and untie you."

"Don't do this, Maddie."

She tipped up her chin, trying to keep her voice from breaking. "You don't believe I can bring him in by myself. Neither do my father and brothers. But I've got to prove it to myself, if no one else. I've dreamed about it for too long to compromise now."

"I'm not talking about compromise. I'm talking about protection!"

"I know. Because you don't believe I can do this job on my own."

"That's not true."

She braced one hand on the doorframe. "I have to go."

"You still don't trust me," he said, his voice filled with hurt and disappointment. "Even after..."

"I want to," she whispered, her love for him weakening her resolve. But she'd set out to bring the Kissing Bandit to justice on her own. And now she had to finish the job. No matter what it cost her.

"Goodbye, Tanner." She whirled around and headed out the door, tears welling in her eyes.

"Maddie, wait!"

A sob caught in her throat as she heaved Cabe off the porch with more force than necessary, then pulled him down the steps and shoved him into the back seat of her car. When he started hollering about mistreatment, she ripped off another piece of duct tape and slapped it over his mouth. Then she pulled the wedding ring off her finger and stuffed it in his shirt pocket. Her marriage charade with Tanner was over. After the way she'd left him, the odds were good that he'd never want to see her again.

Maddie started the engine before she could change her mind, then peeled out of town, leaving both Tanner and her heart behind.

16

TANNER SAT TIED TO THE chair as long shadows stretched across the living room of his grandmother's house. Both of his arms had gone numb an hour ago. But he knew he had only himself to blame for his predicament.

He licked his lips, still tasting the salt from Maddie's tears. The pain in her voice had been real. He remembered the story she'd told him about boarding school, about her father sending her away after her mother's death. No doubt she knew about loneliness, too.

Tanner wished he had it all to do over again. Wished he could go back twenty-four hours ago when Maddie was warm and loving in his arms. Instead of abandoning her at dawn, he could have gently woken her with his kisses. They could have worked out a plan together.

Instead, he'd loved and left her, just as she'd accused. His heart contracted when he thought about her waking up alone this morning. That stupid note on his pillow. The initial fear she must have felt that he'd used her. Hell, what else was she supposed to think?

Tanner had blown it. The woman he loved had seen him trussed to a chair with rainbow-colored yarn. He'd wanted to play the hero and had ended up in the fool's role.

And he'd played it to the hilt.

You don't believe in me. Her words echoed in his head. He just wished he could be given another chance to prove to her that it wasn't true.

An hour later, headlights shone in the window. Hope sparked within him that he might have another chance. Maybe Maddie had come back for him.

Only it wasn't Maddie who kicked in the door.

Tanner squinted in the darkness, searching for a badge on the man who barreled into the house, gun drawn.

The intruder pointed it at him. "Who are you?"

"Tanner Blackburn," he replied. "Are you the sheriff?"

"No." The man smiled. "I'm your worst nightmare."

"Could you be a little more specific?" he asked, watching the man holster his gun.

"The name is Griffin. Tate Griffin." He walked toward the chair. "Who tied you up?"

"None of your business." He didn't see much of a resemblance between Maddie and her brother. For one thing, the man weighed a good two hundred and fifty pounds. For another, he was all muscle, with none of Maddie's softness. He didn't seem as intelligent, either.

And that might be a point in Tanner's favor.

"Would you mind untying me?" he asked.

Tate glared at him. "Yes, as a matter of fact, I would." Then he called over his shoulder. "Ben, get in here!"

Another hulk of a man entered through the kitchen. He looked at Tanner, his brow furrowed. "Why the hell did you tie him up?"

"I didn't," Tate replied, hitching one foot up on the ottoman. "He was like that when I got here."

"Where's Maddie?" Ben asked, looking around the living room.

"I don't know." Tate started roaming through the house. "But I don't think she's here."

"Did you check upstairs?"

"Not yet."

"She's not here," Tanner said, watching as Ben headed for the staircase.

They both ignored him.

Tate waited until his brother returned. "Well?"

"She's not up there. But guess what I found?"

"What?"

"This." Ben held up a pair of men's leopard print thong underwear that must belong to Cabe. "Looks like lover boy here is ready for action."

"You've got it all wrong," Tanner countered. "I'm not the Kissing Bandit."

"Right," Tate said with a snort. "You just happen to have the same name as the Kissing Bandit. Give it up, Blackburn. We tracked you and Maddie here. Now the only question is, where is our sister?"

Tanner opened his mouth, then closed it again.

"What's wrong, Blackburn?" Ben chided. "Don't you kiss and tell?"

"We know you were with Maddie," Tate said, his voice deceptively calm, even as his brown eyes blazed with anger. "We know that you spent the last three days in a place called Crab Orchard."

"And nights," Ben interjected.

"Alone in a room with her. We talked to the land-lady of the bed-and-breakfast. She was very concerned when she heard you were a fugitive."

"And her dog bit me," Ben said, rubbing his left hand.

Tanner smiled. *Score one for Harry.*

"If you touched one hair on our sister's head," Tate began, his beefy hands clenching into fists.

Despite his predicament, Tanner could empathize with the Griffin boys. He felt the same way about his own sister. But he wasn't about to tell them where to find Maddie. He was still as worried as hell about her, but he wouldn't let her brothers take away her dream. Not when it meant so much to her.

Tate stood up. "Time is not on your side, Blackburn. And we're not going anywhere until you tell us what we want to know."

"I'm not telling you anything."

Ben stepped forward. "That landlady in Crab Orchard told us you two were married. That's a lie, isn't it?"

Tanner blinked. "Maddie and I only met a week ago. Do you really think she'd marry me in such a short time?"

Ben and Tate looked at each other. Then Tate shook his head. "We don't know what to think. All we do know is that the Kissing Bandit has a strange effect on women."

"And we found this weird magazine in Maddie's apartment," Ben added.

Tanner nodded. "The *Texas Mail-Order Men* magazine."

Tate's eyes narrowed. "How did you know that?"

"Because his picture was in it, you idiot," Ben replied. "That's how he lures women into his clutches."

Tanner closed his eyes. "For the last time, I am not the Kissing Bandit."

"For the last time," Tate said, "tell us where our sister is."

Tanner clenched his jaw.

Ben looked at his brother. "He's not going to tell us."

Tate nodded. "Okay, cut him loose."

Tanner looked up in surprise as Ben pulled a pocketknife out of his pocket. Then he watched him slice through the yarn binding Tanner to the chair.

"Thanks, boys," Tanner said, rising stiffly to his feet. He winced as the blood rushed back into his numb limbs.

"Our pleasure," Ben said, pocketing the knife.

When Tanner turned around, Tate jabbed him the gut with a clenched fist. He doubled over from the powerful blow, which gave Ben an opportunity to punch him in the jaw.

"You don't want to do this the easy way," Tate said, raising his fists in the air, "then we'll do it the hard way. Now, are you ready to tell us where our sister is?"

Tanner sucked in a breath, ready to fight for the woman he loved. "No."

17

MADDIE KNOCKED ON THE door to her father's office. She'd waited fifteen long years for this moment. To see the pride light in her father's eyes. To finally feel as if she truly deserved the Griffin name.

So why didn't it seem so important anymore?

"Come in."

She opened the door, expecting to be met by Gus Griffin's trademark roar. He knew she was coming. She'd dropped Cabe off at the local precinct over two hours ago. No doubt the bondsman had notified Gus of the development, perhaps even cut him a check already.

But Maddie didn't care about the money. She'd called Hominy from a pay phone near the police station, finally getting through to Olive White's house. But no one had answered the phone. Either the sheriff hadn't kept his word and Tanner was still tied up. Or else he'd already returned to Dallas.

Gus Griffin looked up as she walked into the office.

"Hi, Dad."

He just stared at her for a long moment, looking

older than ever before. Then he stood up and walked toward her. Before she could say another word, he pulled her into his arms, squeezing her tight. "Maddie. Thank God, you're all right."

She let out a surprised gasp, then hugged him back. She breathed in his smoky scent, realizing how very rare such hugs had been in the Griffin family. Her father wasn't a demonstrative man, but she could feel the shudder that passed through him as he held her.

"I'm fine, Dad," she whispered, tears stinging her eyes. She didn't want to cry anymore. She'd cried for over half the trip to Chicago. It was a sign of weakness. But a renegade tear rolled down her face anyway.

He pulled back at last, holding her at arm's length. "Are you sure you're all right?"

"Positive." A watery smile curved her lips. "I did it. I brought in the Kissing Bandit."

"I know." He let her go, then turned and walked to the window.

She waited. But the words she'd wanted to hear for so long didn't come. *I'm proud of you, Maddie. You're a true Griffin, Maddie. It's time you join the business, Maddie.*

Gus didn't say any of those things. Instead, he braced one big hand on the windowsill and looked out over the city skyline.

"Dad?" she said at last, unnerved by his uncharacteristic silence.

"Do you remember what happened after your mother died?" he asked at last, still staring out the window.

"You sent me away."

He shook his head, finally turning to face her. "No, before that. About a month after her funeral."

She couldn't remember anything from that time except the heartache of losing her mother. They'd all been lost. Her dad, Tate and Ben. All hurting.

"You broke your arm," Gus said, a half smile tipping up the corner of his mouth. "Ben dared you to climb onto the roof."

Maddie smiled, the memory rushing back. "I could never refuse a dare."

Gus sighed. "I know. That was the problem. I'd promised your mother I'd take care of you and the next thing I knew you were up on the roof."

"Not for long," Maddie joked.

He rubbed one hand over his jaw. "When Ben came running into the house yelling that you'd fallen off the roof, my heart almost stopped. I was sure I'd find you..."

She walked over to him. Gus Griffin had been thirty-five years old when he'd married her mother. Now, at sixty-five, his hair was silver instead of brown. The lines in his face were deeper and more pronounced. He was still in excellent physical condition, but his eyes looked tired.

"You'd find me what?" she asked softly.

"Crippled," he bit out. "Or worse."

She reached out and touched his forearm. "I was fine. It was just a hairline fracture. The doctor didn't even put my arm in a cast. Just a splint."

"I know." He swallowed. "But that's the day I decided to send you to boarding school."

The old pain jabbed at her. "Just because I fell off the roof?"

"No." Gus raked a hand through his silver hair. "Because I didn't have the first clue about how to raise a girl. Or a boy, for that matter."

Her throat tightened. "Ben and Tate turned out all right."

"Maybe." Then he reached up to brush her cheek. "But you're perfect, Maddie. Just like your mother. And just as beautiful."

Tanner had called her beautiful, too. Her throat tightened. "All I wanted was to be with my family. I never wanted to go to boarding school, Dad. I hated it."

"And I didn't want to send you away. But I was terrified of doing something wrong. Most little girls I knew would never climb up on a roof."

"I wasn't like most little girls."

He smiled. "You still aren't."

She reached for his hand. "I'm not a little girl anymore, Dad."

He wrapped his big fingers around her hand. "I guess you need to keep reminding me."

"I will," she promised. "Loud and often."

"You'll get plenty of opportunities," he said, "since you start work first thing in the morning."

She blinked. "Do you mean it?"

He nodded. "I decided to bring you into the business as a bounty hunter the day after you called me from Texas. It didn't matter to me whether you brought back the Kissing Bandit or not."

"I don't understand."

"I'm damn proud of you, Maddie, not only for catching the Kissing Bandit, but for having the tenacity it takes to be in this business. I know I gave you a hard time. It was only when you left that I realized I stood a greater chance of losing you if I didn't let you work for me than if I did."

He was proud of her. After twenty-five years, Gus Griffin had finally said the words she'd longed to hear. "I won't make you regret it, Dad. I promise."

He hugged her again. "All right. Enough of this touchy-feely crap. Now tell me how you did it. How did you catch the Kissing Bandit?"

She took a deep breath. "It's a long story."

TANNER ACHED EVERYWHERE.

He lay sprawled in the back seat of the Griffin

boys' Chevy Impala. It hurt to move. It hurt even worse to breathe. He closed his eyes, his head pounding as the radio blared a raucous country song about friends in low places. Tanner felt about as low as he could go.

"Home sweet home," Tate crooned, bringing the car to a halt.

"Wait until Dad sees what we're bringing him," Ben said, opening the back door and hauling Tanner out.

"It will be better than Christmas," Tate declared, grabbing Tanner's other arm. They kept him sandwiched between them as they marched up to a stone-gray building. A small, discreet sign that read Griffin Bail Enforcement Agency adorned the steel door.

Tanner gritted his teeth as he walked, determined not to groan from the pain. His best guess was that he had at least two broken ribs to go with his numerous contusions. Tate and Ben had taken turns at playing punching bag, frustrated with Tanner's vow of silence.

At least he'd gotten in a few punches of his own. Tate sported a shiner on his left eye the size of a dinner plate. It went well with his split lip. Ben had lost a front tooth in the scuffle, and had an ugly, gaping gash over his right eyebrow.

The receptionist looked up as they entered the outer office, her mouth falling open. No doubt they made a startling trio.

"Is Dad here?" Ben asked.

"Yes, but he's not alone—"

"This can't wait," Tate interjected, ushering Tanner toward a closed door. He didn't bother to knock, just threw the door open, then shoved Tanner inside.

His foot caught on the threshold and he stumbled forward, falling to his knees. A searing pain shot through his ribs. He clutched the shag carpeting in agony, a misty haze distorting his vision. He took slow, shallow breaths, willing himself not to pass out.

"Tanner?"

He looked up to see Maddie staring down at him in horror. *Damn.* She was the last person he wanted to see right now. Or rather, he didn't want her to see him. Not when he was literally on his knees.

Tate rushed over to his little sister, sweeping her off her feet and into a bear hug. "Thank God, you're safe. When Blackburn refused to tell us where you were, we didn't know what to think."

Maddie struggled out of his embrace. "What's going on here?"

Ben hitched his thumb toward Tanner. "We got him for you, sis. The Kissing Bandit isn't going to do any more kissing for a very long time."

Maddie kneeled down by Tanner, her trembling fingers deftly tracing the swollen bruises on his temple and jaw. "My brothers did this to you?"

Tanner sat up on his knees, trying to garner the strength to stand. "I'm all right."

She placed her hands on her hips. "Yes, I can see that. You're so all right you can hardly move."

An older man who could only be Gus Griffin stepped forward. He was as big as his sons, but his eyes sparked with intelligence, not bravado like the two younger Griffins. Now those eyes were shrewdly assessing Tanner and obviously hadn't missed the way Maddie was touching him. "Will someone please tell me what's going on here?"

"We brought in the Kissing Bandit," Tate replied with a smug grin. "Only we decided to haul him here first instead of the police station because he refused to tell us anything about Maddie. We figured you could pry the information out of him, Dad."

Maddie stood up and whirled on her brothers. "This isn't the Kissing Bandit, you Neanderthals! I just delivered the real Kissing Bandit to the police. This is his cousin, Tanner Blackburn."

Ben snorted. "Tanner Blackburn just happens to be the Kissing Bandit's name."

"It's one of his aliases," Gus interjected. He folded his burly arms across his chest. "Maddie's right. She brought in the real Kissing Bandit a few hours ago. I've already talked to the bail bondsman. The fingerprints match, so the identity has been established."

Tate scowled down at Tanner. "So who the hell is this?"

Maddie's nostrils flared as she stood beside him. From her stance, Tanner could tell that if she had her stun gun in her hand, Tate would be toast. "This is the man I love."

Tanner looked up at her, a smile making his face hurt. "Now you tell me."

Gus pointed at him. "This is the guy you were telling me about?"

She nodded, her cheeks pink. "Yes, Dad."

Tanner struggled to his feet as Gus slowly approached him.

"So you're the man who handcuffed my daughter?"

A fraternal growl emanated from Ben's throat. "I knew he was trouble."

"She handcuffed me first," Tanner said in his own defense.

Gus arched a thick brow. "Sounds like an eventful week. What else happened?"

"I think that's between Maddie and I," Tanner said evenly.

"See, Dad," Tate exclaimed angrily. "The guy clams up whenever you ask him a simple question. That's why Ben and I had to use a little...physical persuasion. We gave him plenty of opportunities to tell us where to find Maddie before we started using our fists."

Maddie turned to Tanner, her eyes wide. "You mean they beat you up because of me?"

"Hey, I got in a few good punches, too," he replied.

"You can say that again," Ben muttered, tentatively probing the hole where his tooth used to be.

"Why didn't you tell them I was on my way to Chicago?" she asked, her voice tight.

Tanner turned to her, wishing they didn't have an audience, especially three men who looked as if they'd have no compunctions about burying him six-feet deep in cement if he so much as touched their beloved Maddie.

But it was too late to go back now. He'd already touched her, and been touched by her. Despite what the Griffin boys thought or did, he wasn't about to let her go. "Because I knew they'd come after you. And I knew how important it was for you to do the job on your own. Without their interference. Or mine."

Maddie reached for his hand. "I think that's the most incredible thing anyone has ever done for me."

He reached up to rub his sore jaw. "I'm just glad I lived to tell about it."

Gus cleared his throat. "On behalf of the Griffin Bail Enforcement Agency, I'd like to apologize for any inconvenience we may have caused you, Mr. Blackburn." He glared at his sons. "And we'll be happy to pay for any medical expenses and other costs you may incur due to this...misunderstanding."

Ben narrowed his eyes. "What misunderstanding?

I think it's obvious the creep has been messing with our sister. And he is related to the Kissing Bandit. How do we know he's not just as bad. Or worse?"

"You'll just have to take my word for it," Maddie said quietly. "Can you do that, Ben?"

He stuck out his jaw, then looked at his father. "I suppose so."

She turned to Tate. "And you?"

He gave a jerky nod. "I guess maybe we messed up."

"There's no maybe about it," Gus said. "Now I want to talk to you boys alone."

"Hold on," Tanner said, squinting at Gus out of his good eye. "What about that offer to cover my medical expenses?"

"I'm a man of my word. Just send me your doctor bill."

"That's not enough. I want you to arrange twenty-four-hour nursing care until I'm fully recovered."

"Fine." Gus looked Tanner in the eye. "Anything else you require, Mr. Blackburn?"

"As a matter of fact, there is." He smiled, despite the pain of moving his mouth. "I want your daughter to be my nurse."

18

"OUCH," TANNER EXCLAIMED AS Maddie pulled the bandage off his forehead. "That hurts."

She leaned over to tenderly kiss his brow. "That's because I'm not nurse material. I would have thought you'd figured that out by now."

As Tanner lay in the middle of Maddie's double bed, the only thing he'd figured out was that he wanted her more than ever. For the past week, she'd gently catered to his every need.

Except one.

And that's because her brothers had been taking turns sleeping on the sofa in her apartment. Gus Griffin might regret the physical force his sons had used on Tanner, but that didn't mean he was ready to relinquish his fatherly rights to protect his daughter.

Tanner hadn't called him on it for two reasons. One, his instincts told him he'd already pushed the crusty Griffin far enough by demanding Maddie nurse him back to health. And two, if Tanner had a daughter, he'd do the same damn thing.

But that didn't mean he had to like it.

Maddie sat down on the edge of the bed. "You look like you're feeling much better today."

He settled back on the pillow, the sheet pulled up to his waist. "Actually I'm in a lot of pain."

"Here?" she asked, tenderly prodding his rib cage.

"No." He took her hand and moved it lower, placing it on top of the sheet. "Here."

She smiled, cradling him with her fingers through the linen fabric. Then she moved closer. "So I see. Is there anything I can do to relieve your discomfort, Mr. Blackburn?"

Her fingers moved on him, eliciting a low groan from his throat. "You can get rid of your brother."

She leaned over to kiss him. Her mouth tasted sweet, like the strawberries they'd shared for breakfast this morning. He knew in that moment he could spend the rest of his life sharing breakfast with Maddie.

She lifted her head and smiled at him. "Whatever the patient wants, the patient gets."

He folded his arms behind his head, wondering what trick she had up her sleeve now. He knew one thing for certain. Poor Tate didn't stand a chance.

A few moments later, Maddie came back in the bedroom and shut the door. Then she reached up and slowly began unbuttoning her blouse.

His body tightened as he watched her. The seven celibate days they'd shared had only made his desire for her stronger. Not that he would change a moment. They'd taken time to learn all about each other, to realize that their attraction went beyond the physical. They connected emotionally and spiritually. Tanner knew beyond a doubt that Maddie was his soul mate.

She peeled off her blouse, revealing a black silk bra.

Tanner had to swallow, his throat as dry as dust. "What did you do with your brother?"

"Locked him out of the house." She shimmied out of her shorts, revealing a matching pair of black silk panties. "If you listen real hard you can hear him banging on the front door."

"What if he breaks it down?"

"Tate wouldn't dare." Maddie pulled back the sheet, then climbed into bed beside him. "Dad announced last night that he's going to retire in three months. And he's leaving me in charge of the business."

She tried to sound nonchalant, but he could hear the quiver of pride in her voice.

"Maddie, that's wonderful." He pulled her closer. "But what do Tate and Ben think?"

"They couldn't really argue with him after the way they botched the Kissing Bandit job." She leaned over and kissed the tip of his nose, now no longer swollen three times its normal size. "Besides, they like the grunt work best, while strategy is my forte."

He nodded, remembering the night they met. "You can say that again."

"I'll be in charge of orchestrating the fugitive apprehensions and my brothers will carry them out." Her hands moved under the sheet, then her eyes widened. "You're not wearing any boxer shorts!"

He grinned. "You finally noticed."

"Just how long have you been lying naked in my bed?"

"About a week or so."

She laughed. "You could barely move a week ago, much less indulge in more...strenuous activity."

"Hey, a man can fantasize, can't he?"

"Definitely," she murmured, then twined her arms around him. "Especially the man I love."

Tanner moaned deep in his throat as she kissed him. It had been an arduous journey to win her trust and love, but it had definitely been worth it.

They made slow, sweet love to the sound of rhythmic pounding on the front door. Maddie carefully avoided putting any pressure on his two cracked ribs, while bringing the rest of his body to a heightened sense of awareness. He matched her, caress for caress, telling her with his hands and his mouth what he hadn't yet been able to tell her with words.

He wanted her. Forever.

Long after the pounding of the door and their hearts had stopped, Maddie lay in his arms.

"Are you awake?" he whispered.

"Mmm," she murmured, sounding sleepy and satisfied.

He leaned up on one elbow, hovering over her. She looked so damn beautiful with her dark hair nestled over her shoulders and her lips full and red. "I'm not ready to let you go, Maddie."

She reached up and traced his cheek with one finger. "The feeling is mutual, Whip."

"And I've decided your brothers aren't so bad, after all."

Her brow furrowed. "What made you change your mind?"

He folded his arms behind his head. "Well, they did some shopping for me. Set up job interviews at some of the best law firms in Chicago. You bounty hunters have some great legal contacts."

Her jaw dropped. "You're moving to Chicago?"

"Yes, but you haven't heard the best part." Tanner reached under the mattress and pulled out a velvet box. "The best part is I'm getting married—if the lady accepts my proposal."

She sucked in her breath as he lifted the lid, revealing a one-carat diamond ring set on a wide platinum band.

"Oh, Tanner," she breathed. "It's beautiful."

"Almost as beautiful as you." He took the ring out of the box, then picked up her left hand. "You might have captured the wrong man that day in Abilene, but you definitely captured my heart. I love you,

Maddie, and I want to spend the rest of my life with you."

She gazed into his eyes. "You really love me?"

He smiled, aware that no matter how tough his Maddie seemed on the outside, inside she was sweet and tender and vulnerable. "More than I ever thought possible. The day you found me in the *Texas Mail-Order Men* magazine was the luckiest day of my life."

"Mine, too," she replied with a shaky smile. "In fact, I was planning to handcuff you to my bed just to keep you from leaving."

"I'm not going anywhere," he said huskily, "if your answer is yes."

"Yes!" she exclaimed, laughing and crying at the same time. "I'll marry you."

"The sooner, the better," he replied, then he reverently slipped the ring onto her finger.

"It's a perfect fit," she said, admiring the twinkling diamond.

"Just like us." Then he kissed her long and deep, thrilled with the knowledge that he could spend every day showing her how much he loved her. At last he lifted his head and gazed into her eyes. "You're all mine now, Maddie Griffin. And I promise that I'll keep your secret forever."

She looked up at him, happiness shining in her big brown eyes. "What secret?"

"That you're the real Kissing Bandit." He pulled her into his arms. "The woman who stole my heart."

Harlequin invites you to walk down the aisle...

To honor our year long celebration of weddings, we are offering an exciting opportunity for you to own the Harlequin Bride Doll. Handcrafted in fine bisque porcelain, the wedding doll is dressed for her wedding day in a cream satin gown accented by lace trim. She carries an exquisite traditional bridal bouquet and wears a cathedral-length dotted Swiss veil. Embroidered flowers cascade down her lace overskirt to the scalloped hemline; underneath all is a multi-layered crinoline.

Join us in our celebration of weddings by sending away for your own Harlequin Bride Doll. This doll regularly retails for $74.95 U.S./approx. $108.68 CDN. One doll per household. Requests must be received no later than June 30, 2001. Offer good while quantities of gifts last. Please allow 6-8 weeks for delivery. Offer good in the U.S. and Canada only. Become part of this exciting offer!

Simply complete the order form and mail to:
"A Walk Down the Aisle"

IN U.S.A	IN CANADA
P.O. Box 9057	P.O. Box 622
3010 Walden Ave.	Fort Erie, Ontario
Buffalo, NY 14240-9057	L2A 5X3

Enclosed are eight (8) proofs of purchase found on the last page of every specially marked Harlequin series book and $3.75 check or money order (for postage and handling). Please send my Harlequin Bride Doll to:

_____

Name (PLEASE PRINT)

_____

Address   Apt. #

_____

City   State/Prov.   Zip/Postal Code

_____

Account # (if applicable)   098 KIK DAEW

HARLEQUIN®
Makes any time special ®

Visit us at www.eHarlequin.com

A Walk Down the Aisle
Free Bride Doll Offer
One Proof-of-Purchase

PHWDAPOP

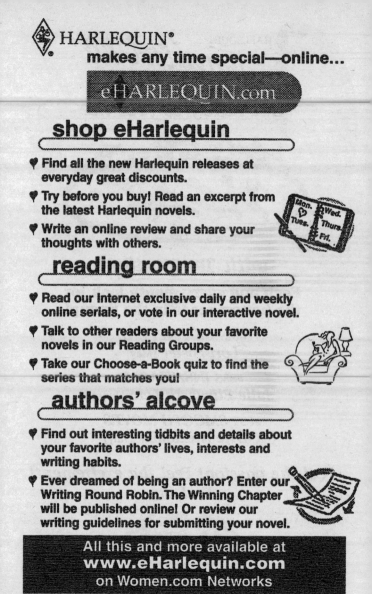